Michelle's Miracle

ROMANCING THE SPIRIT

CB SAMET

AVANTSTAR
PUBLISHING

ISBN: 978-1-950942-56-5

A ROMANCING THE
SPIRIT NOVELLA

MICHELLE'S MIRACLE

CB SAMET

One

Michelle walked for an hour through New York City blocks to get from her apartment in Park Slope to the commercial building for her appointment. The cool spring air chilled her cheeks, but her brisk pace, overcoat, and hat kept her core warm.

When she arrived at her destination, she took the stairs to the fourth floor and walked the corridor to find her new accountant.

She came to the office with the business name on the door:

CONNOR ROSS, CPA

She knocked and slowly entered the office.

A man about her age, mid-thirties, stood and came out from behind his oak desk. "Ms. Barcella, you're very punctual."

The man had dark brown hair and an immaculately trimmed beard just long enough to be a beard rather than stubble. The room and his appearance conveyed professionalism.

She shook the hand he offered as she glanced around the small office appraisingly. The furniture was tasteful—darkly stained wood against light gray walls. A painting of a frosted mountain peak hung on the wall opposite the desk.

"I'm Connor Ross."

"Oh." She dropped her hand. She thought this younger man was the office manager or receptionist. "I was expecting someone older and maybe balding. That's incredibly stereotypical of me."

He shrugged and grinned. "Another twenty or thirty years and you might be right. Although, my father still has a full head of hair, so I've got that in my favor."

He walked around his desk and slipped on a pair of reading glasses. "Are you ready to get started? If you'd like, I can get you a cup of coffee, a soda, or bottled water."

Behind Connor and off to the wall by the window, the faint shimmer of a woman dressed in blue jeans and a pink sweater rippled into view. She stood, staring out the window.

Please, not here ... not today.

Michelle bit back a groan. She just wanted someone to help her with money management—not someone haunted by a ghost. "Maybe this was a bad idea."

"I'm sorry?" Connor's expression turned confused.

"You're obviously busy. I shouldn't take up your time."

"You have an appointment," he reminded her with a bemused expression.

"Right." She glanced at the brunette near the window and back at Connor. Maybe if the woman stayed over there,

Michelle could get through this appointment. "It would be rude of me to leave. I'll stay." She handed him her folder containing the documents outlining her assets. She had an electronic version she could send but wanted to meet the person who might manage her accounts before sending personal information.

"Please, have a seat."

He waited patiently as she carefully took off her hat and coat and set them down in the client chair beside her. He settled into his leather chair across from her at the large desk.

The ghost by the window turned her attention to the two of them. Michelle concentrated on not making eye contact with her so the ghost wouldn't know she could see her.

"Oh, Connor," the woman said in a pitying voice. "When a pretty woman like that enters your office, you need to take her coat for her." She sighed. "How are you ever going to remarry?"

Connor, oblivious to the woman's gentle chiding, looked intently over Michelle's documents.

Michelle's gaze fell on a photograph on his desk. The woman, who was now a ghost, looked very alive in the photo as she smiled and pressed one rosy cheek against Connor's cheek. He wore a delighted smile.

"What did you have in mind?" Connor asked.

"Hmm? Oh. I'd like to set up some accounts with the money from my parents' life insurance policy. I was thinking of investing in a variety—bonds, stocks, and real estate. A sum should be safely earning interest that will create a monthly stipend for me. And a certain amount would need to be set aside for retirement."

"Both of your parents passed?" He set down his glasses, looked at her, and folded his arms on his desk.

"Plane crash a year ago. I'm finally getting around to making financial decisions."

"I'm sorry for your loss. I know what it's like to lose a loved one."

"Your wife." Michelle regretted the words the instant they were out of her mouth.

"Um, yes. Leukemia. How did you know?"

"You have a picture of the two of you here, but you're not wearing a wedding ring."

And I can see her spirit by the window, she didn't add.

Michelle had dodged enough questions around the knowledge she inadvertently learned by seeing and talking to ghosts that she could think fast on her feet to provide alternative explanations. Except now, Connor was probably wondering why Michelle was noticing the absence of a wedding ring. At least that was perhaps less creepy than the conclusion people sometimes drew—that she'd cyber-stalked them and learned personal information online.

"I'm sorry," she told him. "What was her name?"

Connor looked at the picture frame on his desk. "Penny." He dropped his head back down, placing his glasses back on, and looked at Michelle's finances.

"Oh, Connor." Penny shook her head sadly. "You've got a gorgeous woman—who checked out your appearance and noted you're single—in your office and you can't even *see* her."

Michelle bristled and pursed her lips tight to avoid the

temptation to correct Penny. Michelle was not "checking him out."

Penny continued, talking to her husband even though he couldn't hear her. "She's single," she sing-songed. "Oh! And she's an artist."

Michelle leaned back and crossed her legs. She gave Connor a disarming smile to cover her strange behavior. Ghosts had an irritating ability to glean personal information from people. She wanted to tell Penny that the best thing she could do for her husband was to move on and let him have peace. However, she kept silent because if she spoke to the ghost, her medium abilities would be revealed.

Connor adjusted his glasses. "We can definitely do a retirement account and investments. I'll need to know what your monthly budget is, including recurring payment amounts—house, car, student loans."

"No debt. I can send my monthly expenses to you in an email."

"Okay. I'll pull the paperwork together for you to give me proxy to set these accounts up. We'll arrange a day and time for you to come back and sign them."

Come back?

Perhaps everything could be done from email from now on, enabling Michelle to avoid Penny. She could provide her signature through online applications. Michelle felt bad for the ghost and empathized with Connor's loss, but ghosts had a tendency to fixate on ideas and make themselves a nuisance to those who could see them.

"Yes," Penny cheered. "She'll be back, which means you'll have a second chance to make a first impression."

Michelle shot Penny a glowering look as she reached for her coat and hat. She wasn't some ghost's plaything.

Penny blinked in shock.

Oh, no.

Standing, Michelle tugged her coat off the chair and turned to Connor. She needed to make a fast exit, though she found the man attractive and might have considered staying longer if not for the ghost.

"Okay. Thank you for your time. You have my contact info."

Connor stood when she stood, taking off his glasses and tapping them on his chin as he watched her fumble to pull on her jacket. He stepped forward and held the coat up so she could find the other arm hole.

"Thank you." Slipping it on, she turned to leave, but Connor was standing between her and the door. And he was close, apparently baffled into immobility by her rush to leave.

When she looked up at him, he gave a slight smile. She smiled in return and began to regret needing to make a hasty retreat. He didn't move, as if her presence short-circuited his logic. She wasn't sure she minded.

"You saw me!" Penny declared. "You can hear me!"

Michelle straightened her collar and side-stepped the accountant. After hastily yanking open the door, she walked toward the stairs.

Connor stepped after her into the hall. "I'll email you."

"Sounds perfect." She forced cheer into her voice as she waved without turning around. "Thank you!" she called over her shoulder.

The ghost was hot on her heels. "Wait. I've never been seen by the living. How can you do that?"

Michelle reached the stairwell. "It's a curse."

"It's a miracle!" Penny glided effortlessly beside Michelle as she rushed down the stairs.

"No. It really isn't." Michelle had had some good relationships and had helped other ghosts move on, but some were needy and clingy. She sensed the ghost of a young woman, who lingered to watch her husband's every day activities, was in no frame of mind to consider moving on.

"It's fate," Penny added.

"Not really. You need to move on and stop haunting your husband."

"I just want him to be happy. He needs to find someone."

"Happiness is intrinsic. It doesn't come from a person."

"We all need love," Penny countered.

Michelle stopped abruptly at the bottom of the stairwell and looked at Penny. "Well, I can't argue with that."

Penny smiled sweetly.

CONNOR STOOD IN HIS OFFICE, trying to remember what was next on his agenda after Ms. Barcella. He tried to recall the last time a beautiful woman around his age was in his office.

Probably not since Penny.

Michelle was beautiful and ... strange. Her expressions varied from congenial to flashes of irritation that didn't seem directed at him. She was obviously distracted, which explained why she hadn't used but a fraction of the one-hour consultation she'd scheduled.

Then his eyes fell on the hat on the floor. It must have fallen when she hurried to stand and don her coat.

He picked it up, walked to the elevator, and took it to the ground floor. Gaze scanning the tiny lobby, he didn't see her. Well, he could give it to her when she came back to sign the papers.

From the stairwell, he heard Michelle's voice. She pushed through the door and startled at Connor's appearance. When she looked up at him, there was that smile again. Confident and genuine.

"Ms. Barcella, you forgot your hat." He extended it to her.

"Thanks. And please, call me Michelle." She took the hat, their fingers brushing for only a moment.

"Michelle," he said dryly, taking a step back, because the proximity and touch did something strange to his body. "Who were you talking to?"

Her smile widened, eyes sparkling. "One of the eccentricities of being an only child and an artist is talking to yourself."

He suddenly felt foolish, rushing after her to return her hat with nothing else to say. "I noticed you didn't take the elevator. You don't like elevators?"

She chuckled. "I was trapped inside an elevator once with a wailing banshee for twenty-three minutes. Never again."

Connor pictured a hysterical woman's claustrophobic anxiety clashing with Michelle's calm demeanor. Still, it seemed an odd reason to avoid elevators. Surely the chances of a strange encounter like that happening twice would be rare.

"What type of art do you do?" He struggled to keep the conversation going, though couldn't say why he wasn't ready to let her leave.

"Acrylic mostly, but I like to sketch with charcoal."

"Wow. And the paintings—are they portraits or land-scapes or abstract?"

"Mostly landscapes but I'm adding abstract. I like to recreate the landscape of places I've traveled. However, I haven't traveled much and certainly haven't flown since my parents' death, so I've done less landscaping lately."

"Understandable." Loss of a loved one in a plane crash seemed a plausible way to develop a fear of flying. "Do you have a gallery or display in town?"

"Not yet. Putting your artwork on display is a bit like baring your soul. I'm not ready for that type of exposure."

Connor shifted his weight. "Well, I don't have a critical eye, and I enjoy most art, so I can offer encouraging appraisal with the absence of judgment."

"Are you asking for a private viewing?"

"Um. No. Well, I don't know." He'd been attempting friendly conversation, but he had no idea what a private viewing involved. It sounded far too intimate.

Michelle did that thing again where she glanced to one side as though an irritating fly buzzed nearby.

"Thanks for the hat." She fitted it back over impossibly long strands of dark, silky hair before walking out of the building.

Connor stood there feeling like a fool. He was trying to be friendly, but the interaction had dissolved into ...

something. Or had it escalated to something? He wasn't sure.

Probably best he just let that one go. The few dates he'd had since Penny's death often deteriorated into him talking about his wife and the other women talking about their ex-husbands or ex-boyfriends. Younger women were disappointed by his robust work ethic that didn't include weekend parties, and the older ones were embarking on new or second careers post-divorce and didn't have time for the activities he enjoyed.

With his hands in his pockets, he took the elevator back up to his office. Work was his comfort zone, and wilderness hiking was his passion. Neither required an abundance of interpersonal relationship skills.

"Michelle," he murmured, unsettled and intrigued. "Who are you?"

Two

Michelle walked back to her brownstone, wishing the sounds of street traffic would drown out Penny's relentless questions.

"Do you like him? Because he definitely liked you. And don't pretend you didn't notice—your smile gave you away. Were you intentionally try to intimidate him with the private viewing invitation?"

Michelle jammed her ear pods into her ears more forcefully than necessary and held her phone in one hand.

"Well, that's just rude," Penny said. "We were having a conversation."

"We *are* having a conversation. The ear pods are so I don't look like I'm talking to myself. As for the private viewing—that's not licentious. It's a term for someone getting a personal view of an artist's work."

"You flustered him." Penny hesitated. "Well, maybe that's good for him. He needs to break out of his shell. All he does is work, work, work—Monday through Friday. Then, he hikes alone on the weekends."

"Sounds like a responsible adult."

"He needs social interaction."

"So, go find a guy to pester into being his buddy."

"You're the first person who's been able to see me as a ghost. I am *not* letting go of you."

"Swell," Michelle complained.

"Just get to know him," Penny pleaded. "He's a likable guy. Oh! And he cooks. He does this chicken and brie dish that's to die for."

"Oh, yeah? Well, I can make mac n' cheese."

"You do? Gourmet? I had gourmet mac n' cheese once made with gouda. It was soooo good."

"Not gourmet. Add water and cheese powder and mix."

"Ugh. Gross. But that just means the two of you will be a good fit. He cooks, you don't. You're artistic, he's not. You're confident in your social skills, he's introverted. Yin and yang."

Michelle climbed the stairs to her brownstone and punched the key code. "Penny, you seem very nice, and I'm sorry for your loss and Connor's. I truly am only in need of an accountant, and I'm not letting the wife-ghost of a man set me up with her husband."

"I'm not giving up." Penny floated closer.

Michelle stepped back over her threshold.

Penny involuntarily stopped in her tracks. "What the—?"

Mo, an oversized tabby, wound his way between Michelle's ankles, meowing and welcoming her home.

"Cats keep spirits away," Michelle explained. She learned that pleasant tidbit from Egyptian folklore.

Penny pouted, "That's not fair."

"It's how I keep my sanity. You're not the first ghost to follow me home. You won't be the last. Goodbye, Penny." The moment the door clicked shut, relief washed over her —followed immediately by guilt thick enough to taste.

As she fed Larry, Curly, and Mo, she shook off the feelings of remorse. She couldn't help all ghosts, and she'd learned to draw boundaries. She needed her personal space. She certainly couldn't be a fill-in bride just because Penny didn't want her husband to be lonely anymore.

Michelle stripped off her day clothes and donned her painting overalls and slippers. After tucking away her hair under a hat, she stepped into her artist's room where a dozen works in progress surrounded her. She turned her attention to the forest at sunset—barren black trees stretching to the sky against a backdrop of vibrant pinks, purples, and oranges. Today, she'd finish this painting. Maybe tonight she'd get Chinese takeout from Double Dragon and watch Sherlock Holmes as she ate in peace, alone.

PENNY WATCHED Connor's usual routine—office work until after dark, takeout pad thai, unwind watching old MASH episodes, and then off to bed. In the morning, he'd be up at five am for his weightlifting and treadmill routing.

She ached for him, wanting him to have greater fulfillment.

As Connor slept, Penny rewound the encounter with Michelle over and over in her mind. Had Penny pushed too hard or not hard enough? She wasn't sure, but she wasn't giving up. Michelle wouldn't stay inside her house forever, and when she did venture out, there'd be no cats to keep Penny away.

Before she could ponder whether her plans to be persistent made her some type of paranormal stalker, she felt herself being pulled into cold darkness. Icy tentacles snaked around her so tight and cold, it hurt. She found herself on a hard, icy surface, pulling her body into her clothes like a turtle into its shell, trying to preserve warmth. Where was she?

No. Not her. She peered at her hands and clothing, barely visible in the blanket of night and gray clouds. She was in Connor's body. But where was he?

Not in his bed where she'd left him. Hiking clothes. On a mountain then. Freezing, dehydrated, and trapped.

And how far in the future was this terrible event?

CONNOR SAT OUTSIDE on his friend Jeff's back porch with his feet propped up near the small propane fire pit as he watched the dancing flames. "I felt like a buffoon. I took your advice and tried to engage with a beautiful woman in conversation, and it fell flat."

Except, Michelle had smiled—something warm but a hint of mischievousness, the way a woman does when she knows a secret you don't.

Jeff adjusted the volume on the baby monitor. He rolled a small bag of frozen breastmilk between his hands to help it thaw. "You're out of practice a little, but it couldn't have been *that* bad."

"Flaming disaster," Connor bemoaned as he raised his glass of gin and tonic and sipped.

"The more you practice, the better you'll get. If a woman is put off because you're flustered as a result of being a little rusty, then she's not the one for you anyway. What'd she look like?"

"Soft, slightly tan skin, curves in all the right places. Long, chocolate-brown hair. Like, *really* long brown hair. She was all around classy. But she's an artist, and I could totally envision her wearing a white smock and covered from head to toe in colorful splashes of paint."

"Nice imagery."

"Smart too. She already had a half-dozen different ideas for savvy financial investment."

"Wait. What? Did you ask out a client?"

Connor bristled. "I certainly did not. All I tried to do was strike up friendly conversation."

"Right. But if that had been well received, was your next action going to be asking the client out?"

"I hadn't actually thought that far ahead. But I don't go out to bars, so when you told me to strike up conversations with a woman, I wasn't sure what other situation to do that in."

Jeff scratched the back of his head as he considered Connor's dilemma. "Well, it's not exactly like I can take you out and be your wing man." He gestured at the baby monitor. "Oh, by the way, Katrina does have about three different women she's interested in setting you up with."

Connor choked on his next sip of gin and tonic. "I'm not sure about that. I'm trying to get better at simple conversation. I'm not sure I'm ready for another blind date."

A small, whimpering cry crackled through the baby monitor.

Jeff pushed up from his seat. "Well, that's the end of that. Gotta go, Daddy duty calls."

Connor followed Jeff inside his friend's house. Katrina worked as a nurse three nights a week, which put Jeff on dad duty. Connor knew Jeff liked the solo time with his kids.

Jeff poured the thawed milk to a warm bottle and shook it.

"Daddy, I had a nightmare."

Both men turned to see Jeff's oldest child clutching a teddy bear and standing at the bottom of the stairs. Connor saw Jeff's dilemma—comfort the four-year-old or feed a crying baby.

Connor set his drink on the counter. "You take care of the baby. I'll chase away the nightmares."

"You sure?"

"Yeah. It'll be fun."

"Thanks, man."

MICHELLE SAT at her kitchen table eating a bowl of granola and yogurt as she skimmed through the news on her laptop. Her email beeped in announcement of an incoming message.

Connor notified her that the papers were ready to be signed.

"He's up early." She took her computer to the couch where Mo leapt into her lap to compete for her attention.

She pet the cat with one hand as she pecked out a response with the other. "What do you think, Mo? I say we just have him send it via courier at my expense and we'll skip seeing Connor's ghost. Maybe if we stay here another day, Penny will forget all about me."

Mo purred, which was clearly an indication of agreement. Michelle continued petting and typing.

SEND.

She had plenty to keep her occupied at home—her artwork, the cats, her endless internet search for a gallery in the perfect location. She would search, find a half-dozen worthy places for rent and then pick them apart for some minute flaws, all the while knowing that her true reluctance was putting her creations on display. The only person holding Michelle back was Michelle herself.

Three days passed uneventfully, and by the next morning, she needed to get out of her brownstone. She walked two blocks away to a coffee shop and parked in a chair with her laptop, a bagel, and a cup of Earl Gray.

"This place is cozy." Penny appeared in the chair opposite her.

Michelle looked over her cup at the ghost with unconcealed irritation. She sipped her tea before replacing the cup on the saucer. Next, she opened her laptop and began typing.

"Well, that's rude." Penny crossed her arms.

Michelle raised her eyebrows before gesturing at her computer screen.

"Oh!" Penny hopped up. "You're doing that incognito

communication thing." She came around to stand beside Michelle and read the words on the screen aloud: "*What do you want?*" Penny cocked her head to one side. "Connor needs your signature, so you need to come back to the office."

Michelle shook her head as she typed, *No. He's going to send it via courier, and I'll send it back.*

"Well that seems impersonal," Penny retorted.

Michelle typed again, *He's my Financial Advisor. We don't need personal.*

"Okay. Let me challenge you on that. Is this how you interact with all your business associates or only the ones with ghosts?"

In answer, Michelle took a bite of her bagel and began chewing.

"Right." Penny rolled her eyes. "I'm going to take that as a 'no' which means the only reason you're not being personal is because I'm scaring you away."

Michelle shrugged. Penny wasn't wrong. Michelle didn't want to be a weird third wheel.

"I'll take that as a 'yes.' Now, imagine if you'd met Connor with no wife-ghost. You might have had chemistry—"

Michelle frowned.

"—or just a friendly conversation." Penny backed down. "I'd settle for friendly conversation."

Michelle typed, *But you'll be there.*

"I don't have to be. I can give you privacy."

Like now?

Penny huffed. "You're being unreasonable."

Michelle shifted her weight in her seat and bit her lip

before typing, *I don't want to hurt your feelings, but have you considered that the best thing you can do for your husband is to move on?*

Penny took a shaky breath. "I can't."

Can't or won't? Michelle sat back, drinking her tea and waiting for Penny to elaborate.

"I get these visions—dark and ominous." Penny's normally energetic tone turned eerily hushed. "Like there's danger on the periphery of Connor's life. I can't leave knowing something's out there is going to get him."

Something?

Penny sighed. "Something. I don't know what."

Michelle dipped her tea bag up and down, avoiding eye contact with the ghost. She tried to think of words of comfort. No one wanted to think of their loved one in danger, and ghosts could sometimes glimpse the future. But the suggestion of danger didn't mean harm would definitely fall on Connor. And a dark and ominous feeling could be nothing more than Connor dying of old age. What's more—if Connor was in some form of danger, Penny couldn't do anything about it.

"Do you have any more information?" Michelle asked aloud.

When one of the patrons turned to look at her, Michelle sent him a sweet smile as she slipped in her earpieces.

"Cold," Penny said with a shudder.

Michelle snapped her laptop shut and packed her belongings in her bag. She slung it over her shoulder and left the cafe.

Penny kept pace, floating beside her. "Cold and fear and pain."

"Frightening. But, Penny, it's so vague. It could be something that happens tomorrow or twenty years from now."

Penny fidgeted with the fringe on the sleeve of her pink sweater. "You're right."

"Unless you know more, it's probably not something either one of us can change."

Death was inevitable. Michelle knew this fact all too well. Of the top three causes, some could be delayed and some couldn't. Heart disease could be sudden or slow. Cancer, number two, was often an extended process. And number three, the one Michelle was most familiar with, was more abrupt and shocking—unintentional, unexpected accidents with life-threatening consequences. While motor vehicle crashes topped the leading cause of death from trauma, Michelle's loss had come from a plane crash. One minute her parents were alive—riding a single engine plane to Martha's Vineyard. The next minute they were gone forever.

"Are you okay?" Penny asked.

Michelle stopped on the sidewalk outside the entrance to the Sunset Park. "I can't help Connor, Penny. I don't have the power to prevent death or injury. If I did, my parents wouldn't have died in a plane crash a year ago. I'm still putting my own life back together."

"I'm not asking you to be his savior. Just be his friend."

Michelle was certain Penny wouldn't settle for the relationship remaining a friendship. She would pester and persist rather than do what she needed to do, which was move on from lingering as a spirit.

Disinclined to agree to Penny's wishes, Michelle opted for another tactic. Maybe she could help her move on another way.

"Tell me about your life." Michelle turned right and began a long walk through the serene park trails.

Penny's smile faltered. "Where should I start? The day I died...or the day Connor will if you don't help him?"

Three

Sunrise yoga invigorated Michelle. When the weather was warmer, she'd be able to go out on the back porch. For now, she sat near a window and faced the golden sun rays. She finished the routine with deep breathing as Larry and Mo tumbled through the room chasing a ball stuffed with bells and cotton.

She followed yoga with a trip to her art room to work on last week's landscape painting. It had three overgrown pheasants looking back at a red-tailed hawk perched on a tree limb at the edge of a forest. With a chill, Michelle realized the hawk symbolized one gifted in helping others emotionally. She backed away from her painting.

After deciding she'd lost her creative rhythm for the day, she showered and dressed—boots, jeans, sweater, and her favorite coat and cap. She ventured back out to the cafe.

"Connor has questions," Penny appeared beside her.

Michelle didn't slow her walking. Despite a long conversation with Penny the other day, she was still lurking in the world of the living. Unfortunately, the more time she spent with Penny, the more she enjoyed her company. However, she didn't want to be roped into seeing Connor.

"He can ask me via email," Michelle said.

"And he needs your signature."

"Again? I just told him to send it via courier."

"He never got the email."

Michelle stopped and turned to stare at Penny. "And why is that?"

"I might have disrupted Connor's email inbox after you sent it."

Michelle frowned. "So you've discovered your ability to malfunction electrical equipment."

"Is that a normal ghost thing?" Penny asked as though discovering a superpower.

"There's nothing normal about ghosts, but yes, most can screw up electronics at will. Really powerful ones can cause a breeze or move objects."

"Spooky."

Michelle resumed walking.

"Where are you going?" Penny asked, following closely.

"Apparently I'm going to my financial advisor's office to sign papers and answer emails." Since only Michelle could interact with Penny, the ghost couldn't pester Connor into initiating a relationship the way she did Michelle. As long as Penny could only access one person in this relationship she wanted to forge, Michelle only needed to remain professional to avoid entanglement.

"It's almost lunch time," Penny said.

"Is it?" Michelle continued her brisk pace.

"There's a sandwich place close to his office."

"I'm not hungry."

"Connor is."

Michelle stopped and stared at Penny. "What's next? You want me to pick up his dry cleaning on my way?"

Penny chuckled in a don't-be-ridiculous manner. "Oh, no. But he is almost out of black ink on his printer cartridge and the chain general store on the corner carries his brand."

Michelle blinked at her. "Unbelievable."

CONNOR POURED his second cup of coffee for the day. He finished rebalancing two investment portfolios, opened a Roth IRA, and added to a client's college fund. Next, he had a pro-bono tax project for a nonprofit leukemia charity foundation. The work was a tribute to Penny.

By the time he finished the taxes, it would be about time to break for lunch. That would be followed by a meeting with the CEO of Schulster and Morgan Law Firm. If the meeting went well, they would put him in charge of their employees' retirement fund accounts.

Connor's mobile phone rang. "Hi, Jeff."

"Hey, you got plans tonight?"

"No." Connor was up for 'guys' night'. If Katrina was working, he'd help Jeff with the kids. If she was off work, maybe they could shoot pool at the bar near Connor's apartment.

The long hesitation before Jeff spoke gave Connor pause.

"Katrina's got a blind date for you." Jeff rushed to add, "she's real sweet and works with Katrina. I told Katrina you didn't want her setting you up, but she's on a mission. Just try this once more, and she promises that'll be the end of it."

Connor leaned forward and rested his forehead on the edge of his desk and staring down at his shoes. That wouldn't be the end of it. The last nurse Katrina had set him up with had spent the entire evening comparing Penny's illness to her old patients. She'd meant well, but he'd gone home feeling like a case report, not a person.

"Connor?"

"Yeah, okay. Text me the time and place."

No. Why didn't I just say 'no'?

"Thanks, man. You won't regret it."

"Famous last words."

"It won't be as bad as last time."

"Sure."

"Okay. See you then." Jeff clicked off.

Connor set his phone down, but didn't lift his forehead from his desk. His mind raced with schemes on how to un-commit to tonight's blind date—late work, financial crisis, hit by a bus. Jeff wouldn't let him off the hook for any of those things.

Connor closed his eyes and imagined for a moment he was hiking the Great Smoky Mountains. He could almost smell the fresh air and feel the mountain breeze. Zero electronic devices and no connection to the bustle of everyday life. Man and nature. Maybe he could do a small rejuvenating day hike this Saturday.

He needed to keep building endurance for his upcoming trip to Superior Hiking Trail.

After standing, he stretched and grabbed his tie off the

coat rack. He worked it under his collar before smoothing it down.

A knock sounded at his office door. He wasn't expecting company, but walk-in clients were always welcome. When he opened the door, he was surprised to see Michelle standing before him. Her face was framed in long, dark hair, and she wore the same tan coat and gray hat.

"Ms. Barcella, this is a pleasant surprise."

"Michelle. And I understand you wanted to review some things. If now isn't a good time, I can come back—or just email."

"No, no. Now is good. Please, come inside." He stepped aside and motioned for her to enter, noticing the brown bag she carried and recognizing the logo of his favorite sandwich shop. His stomach responded with an eager growl.

"I brought lunch. By the sound of it, perhaps we should eat first."

Connor took the bag, set it aside, and helped her out of her coat. He hung it on a rack near the door. "Actually, this will only take a few minutes. If we get business out of the way first, we can better enjoy lunch."

"Okay. Business first."

MERCIFULLY, Michelle was able to focus on Connor's explanation of each financial document she signed as Penny kept quiet by the window. She'd worried Penny would distract her, but she was surprised to find her own thoughts disrupting her concentration. Along with discussions of diversifying her portfolio, Michelle caught herself noticing the richness of Connor's dark eyes and long length of his eyelashes. Was his hair as thick as it looked?

She glanced at Penny who silently observed the two of them at Connor's desk. Scheming little trickster. But Michelle couldn't really be upset at Penny wanting companionship for someone she cared about, even though she was misguided in thinking Michelle was that companion.

Connor moved his mouse and clicked it several times. "I'll print a copy off for your records."

"Right. Printer." She stood, walked to her coat, and dug in her pocket. "I bought this for you."

Connor accepted the ink cartridge with a puzzled look. "You bought me ink? And you got the exact cartridge matching my printer?" He walked over to where her documents were printing and looked at the faded image. "You're giving this to me just as I ran out of ink?"

"Call it women's intuition." Dang. She should have considered the ramifications of buying him an ink cartridge. "Lunch?"

"Lunch," Connor agreed with a skeptical tone.

Finally, the financial planning ended, and they were reaching for sandwiches. Michelle could focus on eating instead of Connor. As she unrolled the paper around the sandwich, she tried to remember what she'd ordered. Two of the same. She'd distractedly rattled off whatever Penny had recommended while in a hurry to get the food, get the ink, and get the meeting over with.

Connor inspected his sandwich. "You got me a Philly cheese steak, no onions, extra peppers."

Michelle looked at her own sandwich. So she did. "Is that a bad thing?"

"It's my favorite sandwich."

Michelle shot Penny a look. "Imagine that." The petite woman shrugged as if innocent.

Biting into her sandwich, she tasted the savory meat, provolone cheese, and burst of sweet peppers. "That's pretty good."

"You've never eaten from this place before?"

"Nope."

"But how did you—?"

"A friend recommended the place and the Philly. It's not that strange. Don't make it a thing."

"But no onions?"

Michelle shrugged. "Who wants onions in the middle of the day? You might have clients. You might have a hot date later. Who knows?"

Penny laughed.

Michelle felt her cheeks flush. Those words sounded all wrong spoken aloud.

Connor swallowed the bite he'd taken. "No hot date, although my friend has set me up with a blind date."

"Oh?"

Hope springs eternal.

Penny broke in, "Ugh. It's not going to go well. She's going to ask about me and then launch into a tirade about her ex."

Connor continued, "Apparently, according to my best friend and his wife, the world is going to pass me by if I don't start dating again." He took a bite of his sandwich.

"You need to set your own pace."

Swallowing, he smiled. "Right? That's what I try to tell them."

And that's what I try to tell your wife.

Connor's phone buzzed. "That's Jeff right now giving me the where and when."

"Can you politely decline?"

"Jeff is tenacious, only slightly less so than his match-making wife. They'd only let me off the hook if I had a better offer."

For several moments, only the sound of their chewing filled the room. Michelle didn't dare look at Penny. The ghost was most certainly staring her down, silently willing her to make Connor a better offer. When at last Michelle glanced in her direction, the expression was unmistakable—don't let Connor go to dinner and suffer through a woman talking about her ex.

Michelle roughly set her half-eaten sandwich down on the wrapper. "Fine."

Connor startled. "Fine?"

Michelle's words had been directed at Penny, but he didn't know that.

"Private artwork viewing. My place. Six PM." She snatched pen and paper and wrote down her address.

"No, you misunderstand. I was making conversation not fishing for—"

"I know. But I'm giving you a better offer. Take it or leave it."

Connor stood. "I'll take it."

"You can think about it first." She walked toward her coat, but he beat her to it and held it out for her.

"Do you always rush out of people's offices?"

"Only when they're haunted," she said under her breath.

"Haunted?" he asked.

"Never mind." She turned, and he helped her into her coat.

When she turned back around, he did that thing again where he didn't step back. She thought about that thick hair and what it would feel like between her fingers. As her arms moved up of their own volition, she diverted them to his tie. She straightened it and snugged it tighter before smoothing his shirt, her hands lingering slightly longer than necessary.

She took two steps back before looking into his eyes to see a mixture of heat and confusion.

"You can think about it first," she repeated.

"I'll be there. I'm excited to see your work."

His sincere tone gave her a little thrill, followed by worry. She hadn't shown her recent work to anyone.

Hesitantly, he mimicked her and straightened the collar of her coat. Her mouth went dry at the accidental brush of his hand along her jaw line.

"Thank you for lunch." He hesitated as his brow slightly furrowed. "And ... the printer cartridge."

His words reminded her that Penny was watching. The ghost kept her distance and kept quiet, but Michelle could feel her intense stare.

She reached the stairwell, pushed the door open, and stepped inside. She leaned against the wall, waiting for her thudding heart to subside.

Penny rubbed at her earlobe. "You're upset with me?"

Michelle pulled off her hat and raked fingers through

her hair. "You've got me all discombobulated. I feel like I know him because you've told me about him, but we aren't actually even connected on a friendship level. Meanwhile, I'm adjusting his tie like I know him—like I have a right to touch him. He must think I'm crazy. Of course, I talk to ghosts, so maybe I am. I really am." Michelle started down the stairs.

"He wasn't looking at you like he thought you were crazy."

"And you," Michelle whirled pointing a finger at the spirit, "having me bring his favorite sandwich. What are you playing at?"

Penny crossed her arms. "I haven't disguised my intentions."

Michelle resumed her descent, slower now. "I invited him to my house. And at dinnertime. I am not cooking him dinner—that's the wrong message."

"What message?"

"I invited him over to spare him an awkward evening, not to seduce him."

Penny chortled.

"That's funny?" Michelle reached the last stair and slipped in her ear pods before opening the door.

"You are so far removed from anything close to seducing him. You could cook a three course meal, and Connor wouldn't mistake that for seducing him based on the rest of your behavior."

"My behavior? You mean the part where I stared into his eyes."

"That's attraction, not seduction."

"Ah, hah." Michelle wagged a finger at Penny. "But is

the attraction real, or am I attracted to him because you instigated this?" Michelle turned and walked quickly down the street.

With crossed arms, Penny glided beside her. "I instigated nothing. I merely made suggestions. You're both single. And I think your different personalities complement each other. You're artistic and introspective. Connor is conservative and constrained."

"Yes, but we're supposed to discover that together not through someone else."

Penny shrugged. "I'm like a dating app. People use them all the time to find compatibility. Besides, tonight, you're going to be in your cat infested house, so there'll be no prying Penny to blame for anything."

Michelle considered this carefully. Penny pried, but her presence also meant that Michelle would keep her own actions in check. What if Penny wasn't there, and Michelle didn't stop at fixing his tie? Then, she could hardly blame her attraction on Penny's meddling.

Art. Connor was coming over to look at her paintings, nothing more. Michelle would talk about artwork and keep her hands to herself.

"I need to figure out dinner."

"Do you like Indian? There's this great Indian restaurant—Tikka Indian Grill on Fifth Avenue. You can send for take-out. The tikka masala is to die for."

Art. Connor was coming over to look at her paintings, nothing more. Michelle would talk about art and keep her hands to herself.

Four

Connor stood in his office staring at the door after Michelle left. He felt pleasantly bamboozled and tried to shake off the butterflies that danced in his stomach at the prospect of a date. Was it a date? It was a private viewing of her art collection, which could be entirely platonic. Connor decided that he didn't care. It would be quality time spent with a beautiful and delightfully perplexing woman.

He picked his phone up off his desk and texted Jeff, *I have a better offer for tonight.*

Jeff's reply was almost instantaneous, *It had better be a woman.*

Her name is Michelle.

That's all I get?

Connor chuckled as he typed in Michelle's work web address. Her website not only had her portfolio of artwork, but also her picture. Connor had pursued the website after he'd met Michelle the first time and found an ABOUT THE AUTHOR page with a picture of her posed on a rock with a background of spruce trees. Since she looked to be trail hiking, Connor had instantly liked the picture. He sent the link to Jeff.

Several minutes later, Jeff's reply came, *Wow. She's a looker. Artists can be eccentric, you know?*

And that she was, Connor thought.

But he also realized the comparison Jeff was making. Penny had been sweet and as mild-mannered and conservative as Connor. The two women were quite in contrast. Yet they were both kind, and a kind heart was the most appealing trait in Connor's mind.

Jeff texted again, *I expect the full details this weekend.*

Connor rolled his eyes even though Jeff couldn't see the motion. *It's only an informal viewing of her artwork.*

Something better, Connor thought with a smile.

DETAILS, Jeff replied back.

Connor set down the phone. He needed to get back to work and prepare for his afternoon meeting. He re-wrapped their half-eaten sandwiches, placed them back in the bag, and sat down at his desk.

PROMPTLY AT SIX, Connor rang the doorbell of her brownstone.

After the sound of light footfalls, Michelle opened the door dressed in baggy, worn and torn blue jeans and a teal T-shirt with ART IS LIFE smeared in bright, bold letters. Her hair was back in a messy braid. He felt more confident in his selection of khakis and sleeves rolled on his blue button-down shirt. No tie—though he wouldn't have minded her straightening it again.

"You're on time." Her voice was slightly breathless.

"You aren't ready yet. Sorry."

She waved a hand. "No, it's fine. This way I don't have to stand in front of the closet for an hour trying to decide what to wear."

Connor wondered if clothing selection usually took Michelle an hour or only would have in this instance because she considered it a special event.

At her motions, he followed her inside her home. The moment he entered, he took in the cozy charm of her brownstone—sunlit hardwood floors, shelves crowded with art books and plants, and a faint scent of paint mingling with lavender. It felt like a place someone truly lived, not just slept.

"I invited a guest without first considering that I haven't had a guest over since ... well, since I moved in. Cleaning was in order."

"You didn't have to clean on my account."

"Oh, yes, I did. I've seen your tidy office."

"Clients come to my office. It has to be tidy."

"Uh, huh." She walked to the kitchen where she had two glasses beside a cutting board with cucumber slices. "I dare you to look me in the eye and tell me your place isn't just as tidy."

He looked into those golden-flaked hazel eyes. "I'm tidy," he confessed with a wry grin. "But the only reason you'd feel the need to clean is if you wanted to impress me."

She poured simple syrup and gin in a stainless steel

container before shaking them together in ice. "Of course I want to impress you. You're about to judge my art."

Two cats bolted through the kitchen. A light gray one ran and skidded around the corner while a dark gray one stopped at Connor's legs and brushed forcefully against them, demanding attention. He bent down to caress the soft fur.

"I should've warned you in case you're allergic."

"I'm not," he said.

"That's Mo. The other is Larry. And Curly is a calico, but he's shy so you may or may not see him tonight."

"You've got a lot of cats."

She dropped a cucumber on the rim of each glass before handing his to him. "They keep spirits away."

He took his drink and waited for her to elaborate.

Instead, she raised her glass to his. "What are we toasting to?"

"I'm an accountant. We have lame toasts like to a fiscally responsible year."

She clinked her glass to his. "Practical. Not lame."

They both drank. Connor tasted the refreshing cocktail. Cucumber gimlet. What were the odds she'd prepare one of his top three favorite mixed drinks?

"Your turn. What do you want to toast to?"

"World peace. Smaller carbon footprints. New friendships."

They tipped glasses again, but Connor drank distractedly. Friendship. Was that a good sign she considered them friends and they could building on the friendship from there? Or was she drawing a line in the sand—we can be friends and nothing more?

"Shall we look at the art?" he asked.

She took another drink and set it down on the kitchen counter. "Nope. Rule of showing is you feed first. That way your viewers are in the right frame of mind for enjoying your art." She looked into her glass as she spoke and knocked the cucumber into the ice and alcohol. She had long, slender fingers with neatly trimmed, bare nails.

Artist's hands, Connor decided.

"You're worried I won't like your art?" He took a step closer and set his drink on the counter.

She straightened and looked into his eyes. "You're the first to see most of these in person."

"But you'll have your own gallery soon."

"I'm still looking. I've been looking for six months."

"Haven't found the right space, or are you afraid of showing your art?"

"Showing your art is baring part of your soul." A lovely flush spread up her neck and into her cheeks.

Connor had the sudden, ridiculous urge to promise he'd be careful with whatever part of her soul she showed him. "I'm sure they're beautiful. The ones I saw on your website are breathtaking."

"You checked out my website? Taking a sneak peek?"

He grinned, enjoying the proximity to her and his own brazen boldness to stand close. He was in no rush to do anything other than enjoy her company, but something in the sparkle in her eye had him wondering if a kiss could be worked into tonight's agenda.

The doorbell rang, breaking the spell of the moment.

"Dinner," Michelle announced.

She left and returned from the front door with a sack of food and began to unload it.

"You've gone all out. Can I help with anything?" he asked

"All out would have been me cooking. But I wanted you to have an enjoyable time which does not include eating something I attempted to cook. You can carry them to the table and dish out servings."

He did so, smelling the flavorful tikka masala, cumin, and garlic naan. When he'd fixed the plates, he returned to the kitchen and inspected the bag. "I love this place."

"You do?" her voice sounded alarmed. She gave a calculating scowl at the bag with the restaurant logo. "Of course you do."

He couldn't gauge her. She'd ordered his favorite sub and favorite Indian, but appeared to have neither conspired to do so nor taken pleasure in the serendipity of it.

Puzzling. But he'd be more troubled if she'd somehow researched and schemed to woo him on the premise that the way into a man's heart was through his stomach.

He reflexively glanced at his ring finger. Penny had always advocated that mantra. But it had been her peppy personality and adoring glances which had stolen his heart.

"Are you okay?" Michelle stood before him, handing his drink to him so they could sit and start dinner.

"Yes, sorry." He took the drink.

Michelle shifted her weight. "I'll make you a deal. You don't apologize for anything about dinner with a woman that makes you think about your wife, and I won't apologize if I tear-up showing you artwork that my parents will never see."

Connor reached up and stroked a thumb along Michelle's jaw. "I accept."

A ball of fur leapt into Connor's chair.

"Larry! Get down." Michelle shooed the cat away.

Connor smiled. "Are you ready to eat dinner?"

"Dinner."

MICHELLE RELAXED into a comfortable dinner with conversation. They talked about how Connor became a CPA and how she developed a love of art. They briefly touched on the loss in their lives—her parents in a plane crash with Michelle's new fear of flying and Penny's short battle with leukemia.

The conversation moved from there to favorites—food, drink, entertainment, and hobbies. They liked similar things, though their favorites varied. She liked painting nature, and he enjoyed hiking in it.

Tonight felt so good, conversing with a handsome man genuinely interested in who she was as a person. He had a deep, warm smile that lit up his brown eyes.

Their differences seemed like opportunities to try new things rather than barriers to a relationship. As they talked, they cleared the table, followed by entering her art studio.

Michelle watched Connor taking in the wall-to-wall paintings in various stages of incompleteness. Another wall contained a rack of completed works.

She took him through the scenes one-by-one—ocean views at different times: sunrise, day, evening in a storm; horses running on a beach; a lighthouse; forests during all four seasons: lush to barren, autumn leaves to fallen snow.

Connor had something nice to say about each one of them.

"That one." Connor pointed.

Michelle looked at the forest with a hiking trail leading through it. She'd drawn a mixture of spruce, aspen, and oak.

"The way you capture the light streaming through the trails. It looks magical."

"I'm glad you like it."

"I love it. How much?"

She blinked at him.

"This is my private viewing, right? Don't I get to purchase one?"

"No."

"No?"

She swatted a hand playfully at his shoulder with a laugh. "No, because you had three cucumber gimlets and no one needs to spend a thousand dollars on an alcohol-induced impulse buy."

"I had three drinks over the course of three hours. I assure you, it's metabolized enough it's not affecting my judgment."

"The other reason is that I don't want you to purchase my painting as a way to buy my affection."

Connor frowned. "I suppose we don't know each other well enough for you to know I'd never do that. But I think I already have some of your affection, and so far, you've bought me lunch and dinner." He grinned and tapped his chin as he gazed up to the ceiling. "In fact, I could claim you've been trying to buy my affections."

"I would never!"

Connor laughed, picked her up, and spun her in a circle. Just as unexpectedly, he set her back down again as if he'd surprised himself too, and turned to the next painting a beat too briskly

She smoothed her shirt. "That's Old Faithful. Yellowstone was the last trip I took with my parents."

"Amazing colors."

"Thermophilic bacteria. I learned they make the rich greens and blues."

Connor turned toward her. "Would you like to take a hike with me Saturday? It would mean spending a half day at Dater Mountain. I'd call it leisurely, but I need to do it with my full pack on as part of my training for a week long trek in Minnesota, but it'd be leisurely for you."

A flicker of unease skated down Michelle's spine— uninvited and irrational. Cold, Penny had said, and pain. She pushed the thought aside. This was a pleasant evening, not a premonition.

She considered his offer. In the confines of her home, Penny couldn't enter, but on a hiking trail, she'd be watching them. Michelle tried to take the ghost out of the equation. If Penny weren't lurking, would she want to take a hike with Connor?

"Yes."

"Yes?" He gave her a skeptical look. "That took a lot of contemplation and evidence of internal debate on your part. I was starting to wonder if we'd had that brief connection a moment ago or if I'd imagined it."

"Yes, I want to go hiking. And yes, we had a moment. I usually weigh the pros and cons before any decision. I don't agree to anything on a whim. My hesitation is a personality trait and shouldn't be mistaken for reluctance."

"Nothing on a whim?" he asked.

She hooked her arm through his. "If you're looking for an artist with spontaneity, I'm not it. I like creativity and I like activity. I'm a woman in motion, but my actions are by design."

"I don't have a preconceived notion of what I want in a woman. If I had to pick three characteristics, I'd say kind, honest, and true to herself. Although standing in this room, I'm tempted to add artistic to the list. These truly are spectacular."

"See, food and alcohol first. Works every time."

"No, I'm serious. You need to get that gallery open. People need to see these."

His sincere declaration stroked her ego. She had become accustomed to getting critiques on her art from teachers during her college days so she'd naturally braced herself for the same harsh reviews from everyone else. Tonight, she dared to think maybe her creations were worth a public display.

Tonight, she dared to think maybe her creations—and her heart—were worth a public display.

Five

Michelle sat on a bench at Sunset Park, still replaying events from last night—conversation that seldom lagged and Connor's raptured interest in her.

"You're glowing." Penny appeared and glided beside her.

"I knew you wouldn't stay away long."

"How could I? Connor has a spring in his step, and you're grinning like a schoolgirl. The evening went well?"

"A lady never kisses and tells."

Penny clasped her hands together. "You kissed?"

"No. I think we were close just as he was leaving, but Curly decided to streak through the living room and barreled into Connor's leg."

Penny scowled. "I liked cats when I was alive, but as a spirit, I think I despise them."

Michelle chuckled.

"Still," Penny continued, "there was romance in the air?"

"Yes. And my looming secret."

"What secret?"

"You!"

"Connor doesn't need to know you talk to me."

"Eventually, he needs to know I talk to spirits," Michelle said. Even voicing it made her stomach tighten. Telling someone always risked losing them.

Penny waved a dismissive hand. "Sure. Eventually. You haven't even kissed yet. Supernatural revelations come *way* later in the relationship."

"Do they now?" Michelle wanted to ask Penny when she became an expert in all things paranormal.

"Yeah, they do. Everybody has their little crazy side. We all have those strange behaviors or beliefs we keep under cover until we're ready to reveal them to people close to us—even then, we usually start in small doses. You're being cautious—not manipulative—by not telling Connor yet."

"Oh, yeah? What's your crazy?" Michelle cocked her head to one side.

"I couldn't hold my alcohol. More than a half a glass and I had no inhibition. I didn't even dare drink during the first six months Connor and I dated."

"And then?"

"And then we went to this big Christmas party—friends and clients of the firm he used to work for. I got tipsy and started doing the *Riverdance* on the dance floor."

"*Riverdance*?"

"You know the Irish dance and music show."

Michelle shook her head. "Nope. Never heard of it."

"Really?"

She moved her head slowly from side to side. "You'll have to show me."

Penny straightened her spine and began kicking her legs. Michelle tried to picture her doing such a lively dance in a room full of conservative people.

Michelle pursed her lips together until she couldn't contain her amusement any longer, and laugher burst forth.

The ghost swatted a hand at Michelle. "You big jerk! You knew what I was talking about."

"I did. I just wanted to see if you'd dance."

"Well, now you've seen it."

"So, what did Connor do at the party?"

"He very sweetly—and with crimson cheeks—escorted me off the dance floor."

Michelle enjoyed the story and understood the point Penny was trying to make. Yet, she doubted quirky dance moves were as damaging to a relationship as claiming to see ghosts would be. In fact, she could see Penny's inebriated liveliness endearing her to Connor rather than serving as a deterrent.

MICHELLE WALKED beside Connor as they hiked Dater Mountain in mid-afternoon.

"This is beautiful."

Connor adjusted his heavy-appearing pack. He looked like he was taking a week-long hike instead of a three hour trek. She only had her small messenger bag over her shoulder with water and her sketchpad.

"Yes. You should see the place blossoming in the spring

and compare it to the vibrant fall changes. The beech, oak, and aspen are breathtaking those times of years."

"You said you're training for Minnesota?"

He nodded. "I'm doing part of the Superior Hiking Trail. It runs along Lake Superior. It's going to be fantastic. I also want to trek more of the Appalachian trail and out west to the Rocky Mountains—Mount Elbert is the highest peak in Colorado. Forget the nightlife of Vegas, I want to go there to hike Zion National Park."

"Such an adventurer."

"You could go with me." He wore an expression that said he'd surprised himself with the offer.

Way too soon, she thought.

"I appreciate the invite. I truly do. I'm not ready to fly yet. The last flight I tried, I panicked and couldn't get on the plane. I only developed this fear after my parents' death. I know it's psychological, and I've read that I need about six months of behavioral modification and then I'll be fine to fly again. I haven't taken the time to go to therapy."

They reached a rocky ledge where Connor sat on a huge, textured stone after unloading his pack. "Well, there are plenty of gorgeous trails within driving distance of New York. We can start with those."

"I'd like that."

He tugged on her pant leg. She took the cue and sat beside him, shoulder-to-shoulder.

Yes, she could envision trips like this every weekend with Connor. His smooth, easy demeanor was a constant comfort. She glanced at his profile against the blue sky. She could get used to seeing him regularly, too. But the same question plagued her now as with every early blooming relationship she'd had—how to get past the issue of her seeing ghosts with a man who, upon learning her secret, would want to have her committed to a psychiatric ward?

She'd posed that question to her mother who had assured her the right man at the right time would be a believer and supporter of her gift. So far, Michelle hadn't met anyone she felt comfortable divulging her secret to. As time passed, she doubted she ever would.

She had the sudden urge to kiss Connor—something passionate which would convey where she dared to want this relationship to go.

Instead, she pushed off the rock and pulled out her sketchpad. "Will you let me sketch you?"

"Oh, um. Okay."

"No, no. Don't move. You're perfect right there."

He froze.

"Look at the horizon, just like you were a moment ago."

She sat cross-legged, charcoal pencil in hand, and got to work. If her fears were true and this misadventure with a man and his ghost wife was short lived, at least she'd take this moment with her forever.

When she stood, he stood.

"Can I see it?" he asked.

Michelle bit her lip. "I don't know."

"Come on."

He walked to her, but she tucked the sketchpad behind her back. He wrapped both arms around her, pinning her gently and touching the notebook but not retrieving it.

He looked down at her. "Well, when we're tangled up

like this, I'm not so interested in untangling to see the sketch."

She grinned. "Is that so?"

"I'd like to kiss you."

"I'm not stopping you."

When he leaned closer, she met him halfway. His warmth radiated through her as he released the pad, wrapped his arms around her, and deepened the kiss. Despite all her paranormal encounters, kissing Connor felt like the single most sublime supernatural experience she'd ever had. She was simultaneously lighter than air and grounded in his strength.

When they pulled away, he stared down at her. "Wow." He reached up and touched strands of hair over her shoulder. "I'm going to brunch at a friend's house tomorrow. Will you join me?"

"I'd like that." She would have liked to keep kissing him, too, but other hikers starting milling about the rocky ledge.

He slid his hand down and held hers. "It's a date."

CONNOR HELD JEFF'S BABY, Arthur, as Katrina and Jeff set the table.

"Is she coming?" Jeff asked.

Connor glanced at the grandfather clock in the dining room. Michelle was ten minutes late, but this was brunch, not an office meeting. He'd offered to pick her up but she'd politely declined. Perhaps she'd gotten lost, except that was hard to do in the era of global positioning satellite.

He bounced Arthur as he held a soft toy for the baby. "She's coming."

Connor's confidence stemmed from the great experience they'd had yesterday hiking and the difficulty they'd had saying goodbye outside her brownstone. He hadn't mentally prepared himself to take such an emotional plunge with this woman. He'd had to force himself down her steps to put distance between them before he took a physical plunge he wasn't anticipating.

When the doorbell rang, Katrina beat Connor to open the door.

"Hello!" Katrina declared, smile beaming. "Michelle, it's great to meet you." She ushered Michelle inside while glancing at the plastic container of store bought strawberry shortcake.

Connor admired that she was the type of guest who didn't arrive empty handed to a host's house.

Katrina took the dessert. "Thank you. I'm Katrina. My husband, Jeff, is over there. My oldest, Nancy, is drawing at the table, and Connor is entertaining our little Arthur."

"This is a lovely home." Michelle greeted Connor with a kiss on the cheek before exchanging handshakes with Jeff.

The brush of her lips sent a warm spark straight through Connor. He hoped no one noticed the way his breath hitched.

Next, she walked over to Nancy. "Oh. You're drawing a rainbow. It is very beautiful. Is that your house beneath it?"

"Uh, huh." Nancy remained focused on her coloring.

"I like drawing too. Once a month, I go to the children's hospital at Mount Sinai just so I can color with the kids there."

"You color with kids?"

"Yeah. We use crayons and charcoal and water color."

"I want to do water color."

"Well, it can be messy, so you have to get parental permission."

"What's that mean?" Nancy asked.

"Your mom has to say it's okay."

"Mom, can I do water color?"

"We can look at getting you water colors," Katrina said.

Connor watched the exchange in awe. Michelle conversed as easily with children as she did with adults, and her smile carried an instant charisma. Katrina was already looking at her with the adoring eyes of a mother appreciating kindness to her child.

"I didn't know you went to Mount Sinai." Of course, there were probably many details about her he had yet to learn.

Michelle went to the kitchen and helped Katrina pour mimosas. "I volunteer there once a month. The kids love it. We bring these big easels and paints. They leave their artwork hanging on display for a few weeks."

Jeff laid out utensils. "Connor tells us you're shopping for a gallery to rent."

"Yes. In fact, I'm meeting a rental agent this afternoon, so I'll have to leave a few minutes early."

Katrina gasped. "Oh, I hope you do a grand opening. We'd love to go. And Jeff runs a catering company if you're including that sort of thing."

"Honey, don't market to Connor's girlfriend."

"Actually, I'd love help with that. I have no cooking expertise, and it would be nice to serve hors d'oeuvres at the event. Truthfully though, I have commitment issues. This is the thirteenth gallery I've toured, and I haven't agreed to rent any of them." She softly laughed at herself.

"She's worried about public judgment," Connor said, hoping he was contributing and not overstepping.

Katrina shook her head. "Connor says your work is amazing."

"I'm not sure his opinion can be validated because I fed him delicious takeout and alcohol before his viewing."

"A strategic move on your part," Jeff said.

"Of course."

Katrina carried a plate of crepes to the table. "Connor gave your artwork glowing accolades. That's good enough for me."

As they sat and passed plates of food, the conversation continued about everyone's careers. The meal gave Connor a blissful sense of normalcy. Michelle engaged easily in conversation and had none of the initial awkward moments they'd shared in his office. Although she'd been hesitant to start a friendship with him, there was no reluctance on her part since their dinner the other night.

CONNOR HELPED Jeff clean up the table and wash the dishes while Katrina rocked the baby in her arms. Michelle had left to meet the realtor for the gallery tour.

"Michelle seems very nice," Jeff said.

"I really like her," Katrina added. "I think she contrasts

you enough to add a little spice to your life, but you two are both gentle, amicable souls who also complement each other."

Jeff rinsed soap off a platter and handed it to Connor to dry. "I would've liked to learn more about her, but I was afraid of asking too many questions which would inevitably lead toward her having to talk about her parents' death. I didn't want to bring up a sad subject."

Connor nodded. "It's painful for her. And under the circumstances, she's not sure she'll ever fly again. She said she tried once but was frozen in fear and had to leave the airport ... and lose the cost of a ticket."

"But you both like hiking," Katrina offered.

"Yes, we had a great time yesterday on a hike."

Connor noticed the exchange of looks between Katrina and Jeff. It was something wistfully conspiratorial but no doubt hopeful on his behalf. And as much as he was wishing his friendship with Michelle would blossom into something more, he couldn't criticize their behavior.

"Don't you have a trip coming up?"

"Yes, but it's a flight to Minnesota, so I'll be solo on that one."

"Other than a fear of flying, I don't really see any fault," Katrina said.

"She does have three cats," Connor said.

"Three?"

"She said one was hers, and she picked up the others as strays. She also said she keeps cats around because they repel spirits." Connor chuckled, but something about the way she'd said it—too casually, too quickly—lingered in his mind. He thought about the banshee on the elevator comment and the other about something being haunted.

Jeff shrugged, "Everybody has quirky superstitions. Katrina always throws salt over her shoulder if anyone knocks over the shaker."

"I don't want any bad luck in this household," Katrina fired back.

Connor chuckled.

"Well, I say keep dating her and see where it goes." Jeff turned off the water and dried his hands.

Connor's lips quirked. "Thanks for the unsolicited advice on something I plan to do anyway." And for once, the idea didn't fill him with dread—only anticipation.

PENNY HAD BEEN WATCHING the relationship growing without making her presence known to Michelle. She congratulated herself on the budding relationship she'd helped propagate. Michelle and Connor had a certain magical sizzle—a genuine attraction on a physical and emotional level.

Maybe Penny could hang a sign and open for business as a ghost dating app. Surely a single success story was enough to launch a business.

She sat on the highest ledge of the Empire State Building, looking out over New York City. There was no new entrepreneurship in her future. Like Michelle had told her when they first met—Penny needed to move on. She could feel the pull to the other side. A gentle tug at her core. A soft calling song. The transition would be easy and effortless.

Suddenly, a harsh wave of cold rolled over her. She gasped as she was knocked from her perch. She tumbled through the night sky until she dropped onto a ledge. Stumbling in the darkness, she felt cold stone beneath her.

Cold and pain.

Connor's future.

Surely, the only reason she would have the power to see such a terrible thing was if she was meant to change it. Pairing up Michelle and Connor evidently didn't alter the fact that Connor would die alone—on a ledge. Penny had more work to do. She needed to take a deep dive into the future and find more details about this ominous, dark event.

She had one purpose left. One last act before she surrendered to the light.

She would not let Connor die.

Six

Connor mapped his trip. Since Penny's death, he'd worn down boots on trails across the country—sections of the Appalachian Trail, upstate New York ridges, long Midwestern treks.

This hike would be thirty-eight miles on the Minnesota Superior Hiking Trail which ran up the coast of the beautiful lake. He looked forward to hiking a varied terrain of cliffs and canyons, rivers and bogs.

With the hectic tax season behind him, late April was the perfect time to enjoy the outdoors. He expected the hike would take four days and would require a day on each end for travel. For a six day vacation off the grid, he needed to make sure everything at work was in order—calls forwarded to a paid answering service, projects at or near completion, and accounts reconciled.

And then there was Michelle. He was deeply enjoying her company. She was graced with easy social skills and didn't seem to take herself too seriously. She could laugh at her inability to commit to a gallery and admit that her flying phobia was a weakness she intended to resolve.

If she didn't have a fear of flying, she might have agreed to come. He was certain he'd enjoy her company, and she'd likely enjoy the scenery. Perhaps she would have found something new to paint. The thought made him smile. How relaxing would it be to have a new painting of a place he'd hiked overlooking Lake Superior on a wall in his office?

Perhaps hiking alone was better. He and Michelle were still in the infancy of their relationship, and a six-day trip was a long time to spend isolated with another person. Except it wouldn't be just any person—he'd be with Michelle. Vibrant, beautiful Michelle.

He leaned back in his chair and stared at his hiking checklist.

Time.

The two of them had time to discover if the relationship was a right fit for both of them. In the meantime, he could hike and reflect on the delightful changes Michelle would add to his life.

MICHELLE WAS SUCKED INTO A COLD, dark void. Icy air cocooned her, so frigid it sank into the heavy pants and coat she wore. Her bones and joints were so cold they ached. She shivered, which made the pain worse. The pain didn't sit right in her bones—wrong height, wrong angle, like she was wearing someone else's body. Her leg felt swollen like it had been injured, maybe even broken.

She huddled in a ball, terrified and surrounded by darkness. When she tried to look, she could barely make out a wall of jagged obsidian rock. She was sitting on hard stone. Opposite the rock wall was open and vast nothingness. Isolation and cold filled her with a destitute and foreboding sense that she would die alone on this rock.

Jolting upright in her own bed, her lungs dragged in air like she'd been underwater. Bundling herself in a warm sweater and cotton hat, she tried to rid herself of the aching pain from the dream as it wore off.

In her bathroom, she lit a white candle and stood before the mirror. The tiny flame flickered. Using pink lipstick, she drew an eye then a closed circle around it.

"Penny Ross, I summon thee."

Penny's ghostly image appeared in the circle of lipstick on the mirror. She looked around. "Whoa, how'd you do that?"

"Did you give me this dream?"

"Did I? Was it about Connor? I was trying to show you the future I sense for him. Did it work?"

As heat and frustration boiled through her, Michelle tore off her hat and tossed it aside.

Penny startled.

"Did it work? *Did it work?* You just gave me one of the worst nightmares of my life."

Penny shrank back from the mirror. "Sorry. I didn't know what would happen."

"Never again. Promise me that."

The ghost nodded vigorously. "Never."

"He leaves in two days, right?"

"Yes."

"I'll talk to him before he leaves."

"When?"

"Penny, it's four o'clock in the morning. I need to first recover from this fright you've given me. I'll go to his place later this morning." Michelle suspected this was a conversation best had with Connor face-to-face.

∾

WAITING, her stomach took a series of nervous tumbling flips.

Connor opened the door. "Michelle?"

She stood before him, panting from the effort up the stairs. "Can I come in?"

"Of course. How do you know where I live? Are you okay?"

She nodded as she took in his apartment—neat and tidy, just as she'd expected. The walls were a light green which complemented slate colored furniture. The living room was straight ahead, the kitchen to her right, and the bedroom to her left. She could see through his open bedroom door that he was packing for his hiking trip.

"Did you change your mind? Do you want to go with me?" Connor asked.

"No. But I need to ask you not to take this trip." She walked over to the backpack beside organized containers laid out on the bed.

His brow furrowed. "Why would I not go?"

"It's not safe."

"Not safe? Are you saying this because you're worried about me flying?"

"Yes," Penny said. "Tell him, yes, that you don't want him to go because you're afraid of him flying."

Michelle shook her head. She wasn't going to lie to Connor. And how would such a statement play out in the future? Would she tell him he could never fly anywhere?

"That's not it," Michelle said, feeling a cold sweat down her spine. "There's a storm that'll hit Minnesota and the mountains you'll be hiking along. You're in danger." She ran a hand along some of the clothing and the pockets of his backpack.

"I checked the weather, Michelle. I always check before I go. I'll get a little bit of sleet and maybe some wind, but I'll be fine. I do a lot of hiking, and I know how to manage in the wilderness." His tone was warm and gentle, as though she just needed patient reassurance and she'd stop worrying.

His patience and attempt at reassurance were admirable, but she'd felt his suffering. She couldn't back down.

"I'm asking you not to go. It's not safe."

Connor's expression shifted to pursed lips in what looked to be a mix of not wanting to disrespect her but also having no intention of indulging her paranoia. "I value our relationship. I would really like for us to become something more. But I can't drop my plans based on unsubstantiated worries. I'm flattered you're worried about me, but I won't set the precedent that I stay home so that nothing bad ever happens to me. That's not a healthy relationship for either of us."

Michelle leaned against one wall, frustrated at the situation but also understanding Connor's point of view. He was under the misconception that her fear on his behalf related to losing her parents—as such, it was 'unsubstanti-ated' and not to be encouraged.

She'd have to try a different approach. If he didn't believe her, she would lose a chance at a relationship with him, but if he died on that ledge, that chance would be gone anyway. "The reason why—"

"Don't do it," Penny cautioned.

Michelle hesitated, took a breath, and decided to ignore Penny's warning. They had discussed the possibility that Michelle would tell him the truth. This was the moment. "The reason why I know it isn't safe is because Penny told me."

"What?" Alarm and something dangerous flashed in Connor's eyes.

"I can see ghosts. Penny is here. She's been here all along. She's the one who told me to pick up Philly cheese-steaks and tikka masala and make cucumber gimlets. She told me your printer cartridge was going to run out of ink and what model to buy. She told me your address and door code. And she told me that this weather front is going to turn into a nasty storm, and you won't survive it."

All of the color drained from Connor's face. His mouth fell in a look of shock and revulsion.

Michelle had feared that look all her life. The look when someone realizes a person they care about was broken beyond repair. Penny had been right, Michelle shouldn't have told him. Still, she'd have had to eventually. She wouldn't lie to him.

"This isn't funny," Connor snapped in a tone she'd never heard.

"It never is. It's never funny living a life where ghosts

speak to you and sometimes tell you what the future holds." Michelle's heart sank. She could see in his eyes that nothing of the joy and friendship they shared over the last few weeks could conquer doubt when faced with the illogical, improbable supernatural.

Never more than this moment had Michelle hated her gift with such intense contempt. Her curse. She'd helped some ghosts and some people over the years because she was a medium, but did it save her parents' lives? Did any ghosts offer up information before the plane crash? No. And now that one had given her the opportunity to save the man she cared about, she couldn't save him anyway because he didn't believe her.

A useless gift really was nothing more than a curse.

She felt tears stinging her eyes. But she wouldn't stand there and cry before Connor like a hysterical mental patient. She told him what she came here to tell him. She could do nothing more than warn him.

She headed toward the door, Connor still too stunned by the revelation of her insanity that he didn't move to stop her.

"Don't let him go," Penny pleaded.

Michelle turned to the ghost. "You asked me to warn him, I warned him. I sacrificed the relationship we could have had to do it. That's all I can do." She pulled open the door and gave one last look at Connor's lost stare. She cast her gaze down to the floor. "When the storm hits, find shelter. If you end up cold and alone on the rock, call for your wife. Ghosts can bring comfort at the end."

With a bleeding heart and tears threatening to unleash a

cascade, Michelle pulled the door shut behind her as she left.

~

WHEN MICHELLE GOT HOME, she poured a glass of Merlot, dressed in her painting smock, and threw herself into her art.

She pulled out her largest canvas, six feet tall, and set it against one wall. She chose a mix of bright and dark colors. The reds and oranges were harsh and vibrant—anger and heartbreak. The blues and greens were deep and rich—sorrow and pain.

What use was a supernatural gift if she couldn't save the people she loved? Her parents were the only other people who'd known about her seeing ghosts. And the only reason she maintained her sanity in a world where she walked the line between the normal and paranormal was because her mother had had the gift as well. Michelle had the benefit of a loving parent with knowledge about how to interact with ghosts and the living when no one else saw what she saw.

Michelle had told Connor in the desperate hope that even if he couldn't become an instant believer in her abilities, he could believe in her sincerity and her feelings for him. She'd hoped that up until that point, their interactions would prove meaningful enough to enable him to at least consider the possibility of ghosts. But he hadn't. His dumbfounded reaction reminded her of the night five years ago when she'd told her neighbor about a potential fall off his ladder or when she warned an old high school classmate not to get her in boyfriend's car Friday night. Sharing her secret never went well.

Perhaps her fault this time had been mentioning Penny. She could have just left it vague—she sees ghosts, or even vaguer, that she had a premonition.

Regardless, Michelle was alone, painting herself into oblivion while Connor took the trip that would send him to join Penny.

When Michelle was done drinking and crying and painting, she sobered up with a shower and several glasses of water.

Before bed that night, she put on a necklace made of Navajo Cedar Berry beads to repel any chance that Penny could worm her way into her dreams. Perhaps when Connor joined her in spirit, both of them would have peace.

A FEW DAYS LATER, Michelle watched the weather front move across Minnesota and toward Lake Superior on The Weather Channel. The screen showed clouds in various colors representing snow and sleet mixed in an image that was visually appealing. But she knew what was actually happening in those mountains. Somewhere out there was a man who would lose his way and fall to a rocky ledge under a dark sky on a cold night.

She hadn't spoken to Penny since her falling out with Connor. Wearing the Navajo necklace had kept the ghost away. Of course, knowing Penny, she probably followed Connor to the mountain to remain by his side.

Still, Michelle felt guilty. Maybe she should let Penny have the opportunity to say goodbye to her. Michelle took off the necklace, left it on her coffee table, and exited her brownstone. She walked a few blocks to the familiar coffee shop. She ordered a small cappuccino and took it with her outside to walk the block.

"Oh, thank heavens I found you!" Penny declared, her usual neat hair looking windswept around wide and frantic eyes.

"How is he?" Michelle asked, spine rigid as she braced for bad news.

"Fine at present. The storm is getting closer. But I know a way you can help him. I've seen a way. You can save Connor."

Michelle's heart skipped a beat. "How?"

Penny grimaced. "You'll have to fly to Minneapolis. There, you'll have to wait till the storm passes. Then, you'll need to rent a helicopter and fly to the exact location I tell you. Because there won't be a logical or electronic way to track him, mountain rescue won't believe you, and they won't take you up. You'll have to pay for a private chopper, show them where Connor is, and then take that information to a rescue chopper."

Michelle took a shaky breath. Penny had put a lot of thought into this elaborate plan, except for one key point ...

That's a lot of flying.

Her knees nearly gave out. Turning, Michelle walked back to her brownstone. Although she didn't know how'd she manage the flying, she said, "I'll start packing."

For Connor, she'd do the one thing she'd sworn she'd never do again—get on a plane.

Seven

On the taxi ride to JFK airport, Michelle arranged for pet sitters to come out and take care of her cats. She arrived at the airport with one carry-on bag and enough nervous energy to fill a hot air balloon.

After she got through airport security, she paced in the terminal until it was time to board. She didn't wait in line. There was no point sitting in the confined space until everyone else was boarded and the plane was closest to take-off. Until then, she could walk the terminal and convince her body she was not about to board a large casket.

"I don't think I can ride up there with you," Penny said. "Are you going to be okay?"

The last thing Michelle wanted to consider was that a spirit in-flight could instigate an electrical malfunction in the airplane and cause an abrupt drop from 10,000 feet. "I'll be okay," she lied.

Michelle watched the flight attendant scan her ticket,

and then she boarded the plane. For Connor, she could do this for Connor.

"I'll see you when you land." Penny slowly dissolved from view.

As the flight attendant went through her preflight check and safety instructions, Michelle strapped in, pulled out her notepad, and started sketching in charcoal. From the memory of the dream she had, she drew the images of Connor on that narrow, rocky ledge. He was huddled near the wall, looking out over the long, deadly drop. His jaw was firm, and his gaze was hard.

Behind him, the obsidian rocks were jagged and slick with moisture. The sky above revealed the trail of storm clouds passing.

She sketched Connor and the landscape throughout the entire plane flight. With her mind distracted, focusing on the details of his eyes and the sharp edges of the rocks around him, she didn't think about her fear of flying.

By THE TIME Michelle had finished her drawing, the plane began its descent. Mercifully, she hadn't been incapacitated by her fear. Focusing on the man she cared about had distracted her and given her strength.

After the plane landed and she deboarded, Penny waited for her at the gate. A look of relief spread across the spirit's face when she saw Michelle walk with determination toward her.

Michelle slipped in her ear pods. "What's my next move?" She was putting a ridiculous amount of faith in

Penny's planned. If she failed, Michelle would be emotionally crushed. She pushed those thoughts aside.

"The storm is just over Connor now. It has to pass through before you can even rent a chopper."

"No," Michelle corrected her, "it has to pass before we can take flight, but I can rent it now."

Penny gave Michelle a grateful look, and for a moment, she thought the ghost might try to hug her.

"So, who is the pilot that will agree to fly me to my specified destination for a price?"

"Mountain View Chopper Tours. Two days-worth of customers canceled because of the storm. The pilot, Harry Harper, has a grandson on the way, he wouldn't mind a little extra money to throw the mother's direction."

"You've done your homework."

"Yes, well, while you were getting over your fear of flying, I had three hours to investigate my paranormal abilities and invade the personal life of the multiple chopper tourist venues."

CONNOR'S HIKE wasn't as relaxing as he'd hoped it would be. Michelle's strange behavior before he left was troublesome. There was such finality to her behavior, like she truly believed he wouldn't come back alive. And he didn't know what to make of her claims to see his dead wife. That pained him as much as unsettled him. It felt manipulative, yet he didn't think Michelle was capable of manipulating anyone.

A claim to see ghosts was bizarre enough, but why would she go as far as claiming to see Penny? Michelle only stood to lose in a tactic like that. He didn't have an explanation for how she knew his favorite foods. Perhaps there was some evidence of that on social media somewhere, but he couldn't envision Michelle scheming in such a way.

He tried to push those thoughts from his mind so he could enjoy the clean breeze, the scent of pine and oak, the crunch of packed snow and dirt beneath his boots, and the scurrying of birds and squirrels around him. When he got back home, he could talk to Michelle in more depth about the things she'd said.

The wind through the trees came on swiftly and sharply. The air was colder than he'd expected. Dark clouds closed in overhead.

Just a little wind and rain, that's all.

If the weather stranded him, he had a satellite phone. He was only six miles from the nearest town and had food supplies well enough for three days. If the storm turned into something severe, he would be able to wait it out.

By the time the sleet hit, Connor had covered himself in his poncho and continued to trudge through the wind. Still not too bad. Even though darkness crept in, there was little point in striking up a tent because in this wind it would become a kite. He opted to just stick to the trail and stay the course until he reached a shelter.

As the ground became slick with ice, the narrow trail became more difficult to discern. When he realized he'd gotten off track, he decided to double back. The ground became rock, jagged and hazardously slippery with moisture.

Despite wearing his rubber-soled boots, Connor had difficulty with traction. He planted his feet firmly, pulled off his pack, and dug out his phone. He needed a little GPS guidance in the dark to get back on track. He couldn't be more than a few miles from civilization.

A gust of wind tugged at him as he unlocked his phone with one hand and held his pack with the other. When he went to adjust the pack, his footing slipped. He momentarily caught himself by holding a sapling, but when the forty-pound backpack shifted further, the momentum caused him to fall.

He rolled a few feet and thought he'd come to a halt all together, but the rock beneath him disappeared, and he fell, clutching his open backpack as fear coursed through him. When he struck a hard surface, pain shot through his leg, and darkness closed around him.

MICHELLE RENTED a car at the Minneapolis airport and drove north to Duluth and Mountain View Chopper Tours. She realized that she hadn't driven a vehicle in over a year—probably not the best time to get behind the wheel when she was nervous about Connor and driving through sleet. Her fingers cramped on the steering wheel. This was a spectacular time to rediscover both driving and black ice. Since her parents' death, she had stayed in Park Slope, always walking or taking a ride share to her destination. She didn't even own a car.

"Left here," Penny told her.

Michelle took the left and drove up a steep gravel incline. At the top of the driveway, a sign along a wooden fence read:

MOUNTAIN VIEW CHOPPER TOURS

"You're quite the GPS," Michelle remarked.

Penny stared up at the darkening sky as sheets of rain and snow fell. "Storm's here."

That meant Connor was in the thick of it.

Michelle exited the car and dashed through the precipitation to a small log cabin. Behind the building, she could see the helicopter. Was she definitely doing this? Was she going to pay money to go up in the air in that tiny metal contraption?

She looked back at Penny who stood under the open sky, letting the moisture flow through her. Michelle thought of her dream and her sketch and a man on a ledge.

Yup. Bird bound.

She knocked on the door and entered. A man slouching in a chair behind a counter cluttered in brochures sat up straighter.

"I don't have a reservation, Mr. Harper, but when this storm passes, I'd like to rent a flight."

He looked around her. "Just you?"

"Just me."

"Well," he pulled out a brochure and opened it for her, "we've got a few different route and length options. Longer of course is more expensive. It'd be cheaper if you had a group of people to join."

"Just me," she repeated, smiling. "There's a vertical cliff I'd like to see." She pulled out her sketchpad and showed him the man on the ledge.

"Well, that could be the stretch along Tettegouche State Park. It's probably a forty-five minute flight one way." He tapped his finger on the price and scratched at graying sprigs of hair on the top of his head with the other.

She pulled out a credit card. "Can we leave as soon as the weather clears?"

He nodded. "It won't pass until late tonight though. Obviously, the other mandatory condition is daylight."

"Right. How soon in the morning can we take off?"

"Shop opens at eight."

"I'll double your fee if we leave at sunrise."

AFTER MICHELLE PAID for the flight, she drove to a nearby bed and breakfast the pilot recommended. She rented a room and closed herself inside it.

"We're all set," she told Penny, although the ghost had been hovering over he shoulder during the entire exchange with the pilot.

"I won't be able to go up in the helicopter with you."

"It's okay. I'll find him. Look, all I can do for the next few hours is get some rest. Why don't you spend the night with Connor? Sometimes people feel spirits in times of emotional or physical distress. You might be able to bring him some comfort."

"That sounds good. I'll do that." Her eyes glistened with ghost tears. "Oh, Michelle, we're so lucky to have found you. Not only have you put up with me, but you've come all this way to help Connor."

"Hey, we're friends, right?"

"We are." Penny sniffed. "I wish we could have been friends while I was alive."

Michelle chuckled and smiled. She refrained from

pointing out to the ghost how a friendship with Penny when she was alive would have been awkward since Michelle was embarking on a romantic relationship with Connor. Or, she had been, until she'd told him her secret.

THE FIRST ITEM Connor reached for was his flashlight. The second was his satellite phone in his backpack. Unfortunately, he lost half the contents of his pack when he fell—phone included.

Connor found his hand warmers, but they were barely enough to keep his hands warm, much less any other parts of his body. If he could move around, he could get warm, but he couldn't climb with his injured leg.

He ate a protein bar and washed it down with water. Next, he dug in the side pocket of his backpack which contained his flare. He'd need to save it until he saw boats on Lake Superior or heard hikers or saw aircraft. In addition to the plastic cylinder of the flare, he felt paper.

He pulled it out and shone his flashlight on what looked to be a letter. The envelope had his name on it. He recognized Michelle's handwriting from the documents she'd signed in his office. He remembered her running hands along his backpack. Is that when she'd planted it?

Dear Connor,

I know we already said our goodbyes. I guess I had a hard time letting go. Perhaps my presence as a spirit has made moving on more difficult for you.

I'm so proud you ventured to start your own busi-

ness, and it has been a success. And you've made time for hiking—my favorite was the Smoky Mountains. Of course the views on your Superior hike are spectacular, but because this particular hike lands you stranded on a cliff with a broken body part, it isn't my favorite.

You're wondering how Michelle and I knew you'd be on a cliff and find this letter. I'll let you in on a little ghost secret—apparently, we can see bits of the future. I can't tell you what stocks to invest in … yet. If only I had this ability in life, I would have discovered which student was putting gum under my desk.

Since becoming a ghost, I've been quite alone—until Michelle. She was the first person who could see and hear me. She's been a miracle. (She argued with me about the miracle bit, but I convinced her to leave it in the letter.) You should know that her odd behavior has been my fault (well, not all of her behavior; she is an artist, after all!).

Anyway, I think the two of you are a great fit. She doesn't think I should say that because she thinks you won't believe she transcribed this letter for me. She's afraid you'll think she's being manipulative, but I think you'll read this with new clarity. A new perspective.

If I am right, hold this letter to your heart and think of me. I'll do whatever I can spiritually to let you know I'm here. You're not alone on this cliff.

Your Adoring Wife,

Penny

Connor reread the letter several times. The vernacular unmistakably belonged to Penny. The farewell was her signature sign off. He felt the memory of her loss again—raw and hard. The pain eased when he thought of her watching over him. Then Penny had connected with Michelle who'd seen Penny in his office that first day and tried to rush out. He thought of Michelle's surprise and irritation that she'd bought his favorite foods.

Penny.

Penny had definitely manipulated Michelle but not in a negative way. In her way of trying to act in the interest of all people involved. Just like Penny—the schoolteacher who tried to include all of her students. The wife who wanted to do everything she could to bring him happiness.

And she had.

But Connor had crushed it. He recalled the look in Michelle's eyes when he didn't believe her—not even a little. Was there any fixing that?

"I miss you, Penny." He pressed the letter to his heart. "And I'm sorry I didn't believe Michelle. I'll win her back. Can I win her back?"

Warmth.

It started at his chest where the paper rested, then ran along his ribs like a slow, gentle tide. Hypothermia? Hallucination? Or Penny, just once more?

"I love you. I love both of you. If I live through this, I'll fix it."

Somewhere above the howl of the wind, he thought he heard a distant thrum. Or maybe that was just his heart refusing to give up.

Eight

W hen Michelle exited her rental car, the thudding sound of rotor blades echoed from behind the cabin. Her stomach lurched, confirming she'd made the right decision to skip breakfast. She forced her legs forward, one step at a time.

Determination.

Perseverance.

"Looks like you're fired up and ready to go," Michelle said to Harper.

"It's an odd request—a lone tourist wanting to fly first thing in the morning. There's some urgency in you that I don't understand, and I suppose you'd tell me if you thought it was my business. But I can use the money, and I don't mind taking in a sunrise over the lake. So here we are."

"Seems like I picked the perfect pilot."

"She's warmed up and ready when you are." Harper gestured toward his helicopter.

"I'm ready," Michelle lied.

As she boarded the helicopter and strapped in, she looked around the landscape. No Penny. She hadn't seen the ghost since they'd parted last night in her hotel room. Good. She was with Connor, where she needed to be.

Michelle slipped on the headset the pilot handed her and then clutched her sketchpad as the helicopter rose into the air. The tiny contraption shuddered as the roaring blades reverberated through her entire body. The harness felt too tight, the metal too thin. The world looked terrifyingly small through the curved glass.

For a moment, she was distracted by the breathtaking landscape. Bare poplar and aspen mixed with green pine and spruce. The mountaintops were caked in pure, white snow. The lake to the right was a clear, sky blue and stretched so far into the distance to meet the horizon that it looked more like an ocean than a lake. The sun glinted off the surface, winking at her.

When they flew near the cliff's face, worry filled Michelle. It was so vast and steep, she wondered how they would spot Connor. [more description of cliffs]

Then magic and fireworks burst in an orange light. Connor had set off a flare. He must've heard the helicopter.

"What the—?" Harper startled.

"There!" Michelle cried.

The pilot banked toward the flare. He flipped on his radio. "Search and rescue this is Mountain View Chopper oh-nine-five. I've got a stranded hiker on a rock face." The pilot rattled off his location.

As they neared the rock wall, Michelle saw Connor seated on the cliff face waving his hands at the chopper.

The pilot glanced warily at her. "Why do I get the

feeling you knew that man was on that cliff. And if you knew he was there, why didn't you just alert the search and rescue team to begin with?"

"There are policies and procedures a rescue team has to follow. I'm not a family member of this man. I'm a friend. If I'd shown up saying my friend was stranded in a storm and stuck on a cliff, they'd want proof. They'd check hotels, shelters, rental records. Hours—maybe days. Meanwhile he's freezing on a ledge with no way to move. But if we 'happened' to find him on a tour? That's immediate proof. No red tape."

"But if he didn't call you, how did you know where he'd gotten himself stranded?"

"The answer, Mr. Harper, is not for the faint of heart. It's better to accept that you'll end your day having saved a man's life, which is more important than how fate led me to you."

MICHELLE WATCHED as the orange and white rescue helicopter arrived. She wondered if they'd do an aerial rescue or land and repel down the face of the cliff. They seemed to be in a state of indecision as they hovered near the rock wall. Perhaps they debated the safest way to retrieve Connor from the ledge. The icy rocks would make repelling slick, but she suspected rappelling straight down from the helicopter had its own set of risks.

At last, the team seemed to have made their decision. A man in a harness attached to a rope from the helicopter was slowly lowered down as the helicopter hovered. Michelle was thankful the air was still and quiet after the storm. The man was hanging like a yo-yo, and she worried that a strong gust or sudden movement of the helicopter would thrust him into the rock wall.

When he reached the ledge, he fastened Connor into a harness and secured the two of them together. When they rode into the air tethered to the helicopter, Michelle finally breathed a sigh of relief.

Harper turned the tourist chopper southbound. "I suspect your sightseeing is complete."

"Yes, thank you."

"Well, your friend might go to St. Luke's in Duluth. If not, there's a dozen hospitals in Minneapolis."

Michelle's mind whirled with a mix of emotions—passion, longing, tenderness, and fear. The strongest being fear. Did she want to check in on him? Did Connor want her to check in on him? They hadn't parted on good terms. And she wasn't sure how he'd react to her rescuing him. Except, he wouldn't know she'd been involved in the rescue. She didn't think Harper had flown the helicopter close enough for Connor to identify the passengers.

If he didn't know, Michelle would never have to answer a barrage of questions about her abilities. She didn't want to face his skepticism and confusion again. Even if the traumatic event led him to consider the possibility of ghosts, and if he believed Penny's letter, what rational reaction would there be to his eyes opened to a supernatural part of the world he couldn't see, other than fear? Who could possibly want to live a life with a partner who sees ghosts?

Her father had. She wished she'd thought to ask him how he'd managed it with her mom.

AFTER CLIMBING off the helicopter and thanking Harper, Michelle drove back to the bed and breakfast, packed her belongings, and started her car. She had a return flight to JFK from Minneapolis.

As she put the car in drive, Penny appeared beside her. "Thank you for helping Connor. You saved his life. He's on his way to HCMC. They're going to have to fix his leg."

"Good. He's getting medical care. He'll be back home in no time."

"You're not going to go see him in the hospital?"

"Penny, he doesn't believe me."

"But you rescued him. And he read the letter we wrote. It's all different now."

"Do you know that for sure? Did any of this really change his mind? Besides, he doesn't know I was on that chopper."

"Well, he would if you stop being so stubborn and go visit him in the hospital. Wouldn't you want to see a familiar face if you were stranded on a cliff and then had to go into surgery alone?"

"I got search and rescue out there, what more do you want from me?" She couldn't stand the thought of another rejection from him.

"I want you to suck up your pride and your fear and go see him in the hospital and let him know you love him."

"None of that guarantees a different outcome."

"No, it doesn't. But if you fly back to New York, you're not even giving him a chance to prove that he might be able to trust the paranormal abilities you have."

"The curse," Michelle scoffed.

"The *miracle*."

"You don't know what it feels like to have someone you care about look at you like you're not the person they thought you were."

"No. But I know loneliness."

"You can't fix his loneliness."

"You assume he's the only one I don't want to see lonely. You and I are friends, Michelle. We talk, we laugh, we joke. You're an incredible woman and artist. Sure, I started on a mission to help Connor, but I want to see you happy, too. I know, I know. Happiness comes from within. But it also comes from love. I think the two of you have that special spark, but you're both going to have to trust each other to make it work. No one ever said love was easy."

Michelle sighed in resignation and took I-35 South toward Minneapolis.

MICHELLE WAITED to be allowed to see Connor. Because she wasn't family, the medical staff had to ask his permission first.

At last, she was allowed back to his hospital room.

She stood, leaning on the doorway. If she stepped forward and he rejected her again, she wasn't sure she could survive it. "Are you okay?"

"Better," he said, adjusting the covers on his hospital bed. "Because I didn't notify anyone I was in the hospital, I'm guessing Penny told you."

As she entered, she noticed his color seemed a little pale,

and his lower leg was in a cast. "She did." Michelle held her hat in her hands and fidgeted with the rim. The lump in her throat seemed to expanded.

"Is she here now?" He glanced around the room.

"No. She wanted to give us a minute." Michelle couldn't tell if Connor was asking her because he believed her or because he wanted to see if she was standing firm on her assertion that she could see ghosts.

"Michelle—"

"Well, I wanted to make sure you were okay. I'll let you get some rest."

"Michelle."

She hesitated by the door.

"Please, come inside, take a seat, and let me apologize for not listening to you," he said.

"It's okay. I know how it sounded—desperate, clingy, needy."

"You are none of those things. Please, sit. I'd like to hear more about how your abilities work. You saved my life. I'd like to at least thank you for that."

She couldn't seem to move from the spot where she stood. Was he saying he believed her?

Her gaze rose to meet his. "I didn't—"

"I'd know that hat anywhere. You were on the chopper that found me. Please sit."

Michelle surrendered. She pulled the chair in the room up beside his bed and sat. When he offered her his hand to hold, she clasped it.

Connor squeezed her hand. "When you told me those things before my trip, I didn't know what to think. Then, when I was alone on that ledge with Penny's letter, I understood. Or, at least, I understood that I needed to talk to you more about it." He scrubbed his other hand across his face. "I felt her out there in the cold with me. And she helped you find me, didn't she?"

Michelle swallowed. "She loves you very much."

"I love her, too. But, I also love you. I'm sorry if it's too soon to say something like that, but it's true. When you're freezing on a cliff," he said softly, "everything unnecessary falls away. And what's left ... is the truth."

Speechless, Michelle brought his hand to her lips and kissed it.

"And maybe I don't understand or comprehend the extent of your ability to communicate with ghosts, but it's obviously part of who you are. I have no intention of changing any part of who you are."

Michelle sniffed.

"So, can we still be together?" he asked.

"We can still be together."

～

~~ 3 MONTHS LATER~~

MICHELLE HAD FOUND a gallery she liked and rented it. She'd hired an art major finishing his last semester of college to work part time to help set up the show floor. Between painting and preparations, Michelle had continued to date Connor as he transitioned from crutches to a boot to walking normally.

Tonight, though, wasn't about art. Tonight, Penny would move on. Michelle sat on the floor of her unfinished gallery with Connor inside a circle of yellow candles. In the center of the circle burned frankincense, emitting a sweet scent. Penny hovered in the wisp of smoke released from the incense.

"Are you ready?" Michelle asked Penny.

"Ready."

Penny didn't need a special ceremony to shift from this world to the next, but Michelle and Connor did. They both needed different types of closure. Penny had become a friend and had helped Michelle through her self-imposed isolation.

"Connor," Penny began, "I'm so grateful you found Michelle. She's a wonderful match for you and you for her. I wish you a lifetime of happiness."

Michelle relayed the message to Connor.

Connor stared at the twirling, fragrant smoke. "Thank you, Penny, for helping us come together. I wish you peace. Rest knowing I'm happy."

"I'll miss you," Michelle said.

"I'm glad I had a friend in you," Penny said.

Then, she simply faded from view in light and smoke—like silk in the wind—happy and content.

Epilogue

O pening night at Barcella Gallery was magical. Michelle had her favorite works on display, each painting with its own spotlight. Twinkling golden LED lights canopied the tall ceiling. Waiters walked through with trays, dispensing hors d'ouerves catered by Connor's best friend's company. Michelle's art student handled sales so she was free to talk about colors, mood, and her inspiration.

Michelle paused in front of one painting—one of her few portraits. Penny in her pink sweater, gazing out Connor's office window as though still watching over them. A week after returning from Minnesota, Michelle had painted it in one breathless rush, unable to sleep until Penny's presence lived somewhere permanent. It wasn't for sale. This artwork would stay in the gallery.

Connor put an arm around Michelle. "Your night was a success." His broken leg had fully healed, and they had a day hike planned for the next weekend.

Michelle looked around as people filed out of the

gallery at closing time. Jeff and Katrina, having secured babysitters, stayed longer. They stood arm-in-arm, looking at her painting of Lake Superior but casting glances in Connor's direction with oddly expectant expressions.

Michelle kissed Connor on the cheek. "I couldn't be happier with how it turned out, and I don't even know if I sold anything."

Connor's smile warmed her, but there was something else in his eyes tonight—an intensity she couldn't quite place.

"Yes, I did."

"Maybe, you're in the mood to make someone else's dream come true?"

She gave him a quizzical look before he dropped to one knee and raised a ring before her. Her heart throbbed with excitement.

"You're my miracle, Michelle. Every moment I spend with you is a gift I treasure. Will you marry me and let me treasure you for as long as I live?"

"Yes!"

He rose to his feet, wrapped his arms around her, and spun her around once. As he set her back on her feet, he pressed his lips to hers in a soft, succulent kiss.

For the first time in years, Michelle felt completely whole—seen, loved, and no longer burdened by her gift. Penny had led them to each other. Love would carry them forward.dd9

<<<<>>>>

***** QUICK NOTE FROM THE AUTHOR *****

READY FOR ANOTHER sweet and magical romantic suspense? There are so many delights to enjoy! Keep scrolling for the first chapter in the next book.

Romancing the Spirit

IN BOXED SETS

INDIVIDUAL BOOKS
  Romancing the Spirit Series #1
  Sadie's Spirit / Willow's Windfall
  Cassie's Chase / Phoebe's Pharaoh
  Vanessa's Valentine / Autumn's Angel
  Romancing the Spirit Series #2
  Carol's Christmas / Allison's Alibi
  Gracelynn's Genie / Michelle's Miracle
  Heather's Hero / Chloe's Cupid
  Romancing the Spirit Series #3
  Sabrina's Storm / Jenny's Justice
  Stella's Star / Gigi's Gift
  Phoenix's Phantom / Fiona's Freedom

THE CHRISTMAS COLLECTION

Dear Reader

If you enjoyed this book and want to know about future releases by CB Samet you can CLICK HERE to sign up for my mailing list! I promise I won't spam you. I only send an email when I have a new book released, giveaways, or special discounts.

Also, as an independent author, I rely heavily on readers to spread the word about books they've read. If you enjoyed this story, kindly let others know by posing a brief comment on social media or leave a review where you purchased it.

Thank you for reading,
CB Samet

Heather's Hero

When Heather's past catches up with her, an unlikely hero intervenes. But when the line between reality and the paranormal blurs, she realizes she's not the only one in need of saving.

❧

SAMPLE CHAPTER ONE

Heather strummed her fingers on the steering wheel to Fleetwood Mac's *The Chain*. Outside, pink flowers from Japanese cherry trees danced on a crisp Tennessee spring breeze. A few more blocks and she'd reach the retirement home and begin a fun afternoon of repotting plants with the residents.

A car plowed through the intersection, ran a red light, and crashed into Heather's Honda Accord. Her body tensed on impact, but she had no time to avoid the collision. The sickening sound of crunching metal and shattering glass was followed by the smell of gasoline and burnt rubber.

When Heather opened her eyes, the world around her took a moment to stop moving. She loosened her white-knuckled grip on the steering wheel and blinked at the deployed, side-impact airbag.

Through the shattered windshield, she saw a familiar shape climb out of the car that had hit hers. Black pants, black shirt, and that walk. Her brain tried. to make sense of the impossible. Blake had found her.

Her pulse snapped into a frantic rhythm. For a moment she couldn't breathe—not from the airbag, not from the crash, but from pure, bone-deep terror she thought she'd left behind in another state.

"Hey, man? You okay?" A bystander approached Blake.

As a crowd of bystanders began to gather, Heather's attacker abruptly turned and stalked away from the scene of his crime.

"You need to get out of your car right now."

Heather jolted when a man appeared beside her in the passenger seat. She'd been driving alone, hadn't she?

He was early-thirties with dark hair and sharp, defined facial features—chiseled jaw and ruddy cheekbones. His brown hair and thick eyebrows accentuated a pair of warm brown eyes.

"What?"

"You're leaking oil," he said. "When that ignites and combines with the fertilizer in your back seat, your whole car will go up in flames."

She noticed his clothing—a well-worn, fire-retardant black uniform with yellow reflective stripes. Firefighter.

How had he gotten here so fast after the crash? And how had he managed to get *inside* the car?

His sleeve had a circular patch with a raven against a blue sky sewn into it.

The heat in the car intensified.

"Move it, Phillips!" the fireman barked at her.

She fumbled free from her seatbelt before shoving open the driver-side door and clamoring out, dragging her purse with her.

With the movement, she felt pain for the first time since the collision. Her left shoulder throbbed in rhythm with her head. She stumbled to a nearby sidewalk on the corner of Crossland Avenue and Cumberland Drive. As she looked around, she didn't see the firefighter. She didn't see Blake either.

Her car burst into flame, and she gaped at the sudden heat and fire. Ten seconds earlier and she'd have been toast. Where had the man who'd saved her gone? He'd mysteriously vanished.

Suddenly nauseated, she sat on the cold concrete and put her head between her knees.

"Are you okay, young lady? Your head's bleeding. I called an ambulance."

She looked up to see a man in his sixties standing over her with a worried expression. A friendly Good Samaritan, she deduced immediately. She looked down at her baby blue turtleneck, stained with drops of blood from her head wound.

"I'm okay." She'd had worse. Blake had done worse. And he'd probably be back to finish what he'd started.

Heather looked around again. "Where's the fire department?" She didn't see the fireman's truck or hear sirens.

"They should be here soon. The Clarksville Fire Rescue station is just a few blocks away from here. I've got a first aid kit in my car if you want me to clean that up a bit."

"No. Thanks. I need to make some phone calls."

She pulled her phone out of her purse and called her friend Evelyn.

By late afternoon, Heather had arrived home to the cheerful yips of Denver. The large German Shepherd greeted her at the door as his ferocious tail wagged the entire back half of his furry body.

She dropped her purse on the entry table and deactivated and reset the alarm before sinking her fingers into soft fur. Lowering herself to the floor, she let the dog smother her with love.

After the accident—no, *crash*, there had been nothing *accidental* about Blake careening into her car—Heather had watched the fire department drown her car, answered police questions, and turned down an ambulance trip to the ER. She didn't need another trauma evaluation—one more CT scan of her head in her lifetime and she'd start glowing in the dark. Besides, she'd been beaten and bruised enough to know when she needed to take a few ibuprofen and sleep it off.

She hadn't lost consciousness after the crash, which was reassuring. Though maybe she had hallucinated. She'd seen a man in her car when he couldn't have gotten in through the smashed passenger-side door or through the broken windshield. She'd seen the firefighter even though the fire truck hadn't arrived on the scene yet.

"Well, boy," she scratched behind Denver's ears, "if I'm going to hallucinate a fireman who saves my life, he might as well be drop-dead gorgeous."

"Thanks."

Heather startled. She looked up to see the same man standing in her living room with his arms crossed.

She shot to her feet. "How'd you get in here?"

Denver cocked his head to one side, looking at her while not seeming to notice the uninvited guest. Normally, her guard dog was very protective.

"I'm not sure exactly." The man wore a slightly bemused expression and the same black gear as in her car. His black and yellow uniform was different than the grayish-brown gear she'd seen on the Clarksville firefighters.

Backing away, she pressed herself against her front door. "I don't know whether to scream or thank you."

"I don't require gratitude for doing my job, and I'd prefer you not scream."

Something about his appearance seemed odd. She stared harder at him and realized she could see her television on the opposite wall *through* him. She walked closer, inspecting him. Denver followed her before walking right through the man to go lay on his rug in the living room.

Heather shrieked, recoiled back, bumped the table beside the couch, and barely caught her lamp before it fell over.

"Nice catch."

After setting the lamp upright, she backed away toward the kitchen, stammering, "You're a ghost!"

"Seems that way." He frowned.

Did he not know he was a ghost? And since when were ghosts *real*?

"I must've hit my head *really* hard." She snatched a glass from her cupboard and poured herself orange juice from the refrigerator. She glanced at Denver again, who made no response to the sound of a deep male voice in his house.

The fireman looked down at his appearance. "I could be a figment of your imagination, but I *feel* like I'm my own person—in a manner of speaking."

Heather drank the juice, the cold liquid hitting her empty stomach with a revitalizing burst. After a moment, her heart returned to a normal rhythm. "Do you have a name?"

"I—I don't know." His expression changed from confused to deeply sad.

She decidedly didn't like seeing him sad. She preferred playful and bemused over sad.

"What does the raven symbolize?" she asked.

He looked at the patch sewn onto his uniform. "Reckoning. Rebirth. Protection. Guidance. They mean different things to different religions. Sometimes different things in the same religion."

"Okay. Let's call you Rave."

He grinned, his warm eyes radiating amicably. "I like that."

She pulled a container of Ramen noodles from her pantry, peeled the lid back, and added water. She hadn't eaten all day. Maybe some food would put an end to her overactive imagination.

"So, you make a habit of saving women in car crashes?" She eyed him nervously.

"I've rescued a few, though I think I was still living at the time. It's all a little fuzzy."

"Yeah? I can relate." She pointed to the bandage on her forehead. After punching the microwave buttons, she hit START.

"Are you okay?" Rave asked.

"Since I'm talking to a fireman's ghost, probably not. But since you're the best-looking thing in my disastrous life right now and you saved my life, I'm just going to roll with it. I'm not going to look a gift ghost in the mouth."

"Disastrous?" he said, cutting through her attempt to lighten the mood.

"How much of the crash did you see?"

"Just you in the car, the smoke, and the fertilizer."

"And my name? You called me Phillips."

"Heather Phillips. I don't know why I know your name and not my own."

She'd never met Rave. She would've remembered that face and those caring eyes. With all of her prior injuries, she'd never hit her head so hard that she saw a man in her house. Why a fireman? She didn't have a fetish she was aware of. Though, if Rave stuck around, she might develop one. Except, she'd sworn off men after Blake.

"Are you okay?" Rave asked again.

Heather blinked and watched a tear fall into her noodles as she mixed them. "Yeah." She sniffed. "Long day."

"A long day doesn't make a disastrous life."

"Maybe disastrous is too strong. No. It's probably accurate. The man who rammed his car into mine and then ran off is my abusive ex. Apparently he's found me even after I moved cross-country, stayed off social media, and died my brown hair red." She ate her noodles.

Rave stiffened. "So, he's still out there?"

"Oh, yeah, he's definitely still out there."

<<CONTINUE THE NOVELLA>>

www.ingramcontent.com/pod-product-compliance
Lightning Source LLC
Chambersburg PA
CBHW022043170626
46808CB00003B/1338